Summer's Island

The Fantasy Maker Series

Cricket Rohman

Cover Design by Sweet 'N Spicy Designs

ISBN: 978-1-7355672-3-5

Ebook ISBN: 978-1-7355672-2-8

The book Summer's Island is dedicated to:
Those looking for Love
Those with the perseverance to Survive
Richard and Yvonne Rohmann for taking me on my first
ocean cruise.

Acknowledgments

Each person named below contributed to the creation or completion of this novel—from offering encouragement and inspiration to supplying feedback and editing.

My heartfelt gratitude goes out to: Sharon Erb, Paul Hodo, Bonny Milne, Jaycee DeLorenzo, and Jerry Gallegos.

Chapter One

Summer

School's out for the summer, but not everyone was happy about that. The middle school students cheered loudly, joyfully, as they bolted from the building to begin their vacations with or without their parents. The school board had voted to eliminate all classes, including the swim team, until next fall. Yes, school was out, and Summer Sinclair was out too. Out of luck, out of a job, and in a couple of weeks, she'd be out of just about everything.

This had never happened before. Sure, she'd juggled the small amounts of money she earned as a part-time teaching assistant and subsidized that meager income by coaching the swim team after school. It was always difficult, but she'd managed. How would she survive the next three months without a paycheck?

JD

JD Middleton hurried to The Watering Hole, knowing that Ben, Chuck, and Ralph would give him a hard time for being late. His obsession and passion for his career overshadowed every aspect of his life. There was no such thing as a love interest. He'd sworn off women. He liked them just fine, but they were a distraction he chose to avoid for now.

"Look who's here. The only guy in the whole world who spends an hour cooking a three-minute egg." Ben, the party animal of the group, was first to get his dig in.

"Yeah," Chuck added, "and who cooks food we can't even pronounce."

They all laughed as Ralph filled a tall, frosty glass of beer for JD. He had some catching up to do.

"Sorry, guys. The weekend sous chef called in sick, and I had to cover for him for a couple of hours." A few smirks and an eye roll let JD know that the guys were not impressed. He always had an excuse for being late or standing them up. But in his defense, the excuses were valid. He took his job and his career seriously.

His beer glass was half empty when the odd expressions on his friends' faces gained his attention. He glanced from Ben to Ralph, his eyes resting on Chuck.

"Okay. What's up?" He waited for an answer, but all he got were up-to-no-good grins. "I mean it. What's going on here?" They let him stew.

JD had claimed on multiple occasions that he was an intuitive guy, practically a mind reader. Tired from his extra-long work day, JD was annoyed by their childish behavior. To make matters worse, no hints of what they were hiding filtered into his thoughts.

As JD watched, Ben, with exaggerated ceremony, unfolded a sheet of glossy-colored paper, cleared his throat, and read the words out loud. "The Fantasy Maker is Looking for a Few Good Men."

The guys all nodded, then looked up and stared at JD. Apparently, the ball was in his court, but he had no idea what game they were playing.

Eyebrows raised, JD shook his head and poured himself another beer. "So? What does this have to do with me?"

Ben explained that his girlfriend had found the advertisement in a travel magazine. Immediately, she thought of JD and his workaholic ways. Curious, JD played along.

"Okay, but who is this fantasy maker, and what would the *good men* be expected to do?"

"We don't know, but we want to find out. There's a phone number you can call for more information." Ben's enthusiasm had *prank* written all over it. "Come on, JD. Make the call. Let's check it out." Three out of four heads nodded their agreement.

Although JD was skeptical, he was also intrigued. Was this a job application? An escort service? Something illegal? What if it was something like the old TV show *Fantasy Island*? No. That would be too good to be true. His buddies kept egging him on to make the call. When the second pitcher of beer was empty, Chuck dared him to do it.

JD double-dared back and picked up his phone. The three men hesitated, but one by one each man picked up his smartphone and tapped in the phone number. A recorded message said, "Thank you for calling The Fantasy Maker. Please leave your email or snail mail address. An application will be sent to you in the near future."

Staring at each other, they paused. With shrugs and nods of approval, the four men keyed in their email addresses. A round of high-fives followed. If any one of them experienced edgy anticipation, he was too macho to express his doubt. They pushed back their chairs, preparing to head out, when a chorus of pings, dings, and buzzes sounded from all four phones. Their applications from The Fantasy Maker had arrived. Instead of leaving, they remained in their seats.

Chuck said, "Hey, JD. You're going to fill it out, right?"

Before answering, JD took a deep breath and blew it out. "Maybe. I have to read it first. And don't forget this was a double dare, so if we do this crazy thing, you guys must send your applications in first."

"Okay, smartass," said Ben. "Let's meet here

tomorrow with our filled-out applications. We'll hit our SEND buttons together. What time works for you, JD?"

"Tomorrow evening? Eight o'clock should be okay."

From the corner of his eye, he thought he saw his friends wink at each other. No, that couldn't be. None of them was the winking type.

Chapter Two

JD

While spinning the tires of his stationary bike and working up a sweat, JD read the application. As expected, it asked for his name, age, and marital status. The gender box had only two choices, male or female, which was okay with him. That's all he needed, though it struck him as odd. Not many gender options for these modern days and changing times.

The first question asked for his preferred location for his fantasy. That was easy, somewhere tropical. Question number two required a list of desired activities. Again, easy. Sleeping, eating, fishing, and exploring. For question three, he was to submit a list of *must-haves*. He stopped peddling the bike immediately. Was this a waste of time? A weird joke his friends had cooked up? Maybe they were all being played. Only time would tell. *What the hell? I've got nothing to lose, and I won't be selected anyway.*

The question asking him to state his *must-haves* was simple to answer too. He'd be happy with a few palm trees, warm weather, and restful, quiet solitude. He added that one evening of fireworks lighting up the night sky would be nice. JD loved fireworks. One night a year was not nearly enough, and he often missed that night due to his work schedule.

Question number three was the last of the easy questions. Question four asked if his fantasy required someone of the opposite or same sex. There were four choices: 1. Yes, a female. 2. Yes, a male. 3. Any companion would be nice. And 4. No other people. *If I answer yes to number one, does a hooker show up?* He chose choice number 4. He desired solitude and freedom from the complications the presence of a woman or anyone would bring. And some alone time away from work was just what he needed.

The last question asked him to rank how adventurous he was on a scale of 1-5. He wanted to respond, "It depends," but that wasn't listed as a choice. In the kitchen, he was a five. Everywhere else, the number was far lower. Not wanting to appear adventureless or dull, he gave himself a four, even though a two was closer to the truth. He hoped he wouldn't regret his little lie. With the questions answered, he was ready for tomorrow night's meeting with Ben, Chuck, and Ralph.

. . .

JD was the first to arrive. He wanted to get this ridiculous project completed and put to rest. He was scheduled to work a double shift at the restaurant tomorrow. His impatient thoughts were interrupted by a commotion coming through the door. *Ready or not, here they come.* By the looks of enthusiasm smeared all over his friends' faces, they were into this fantasy maker opportunity, real or not. Or else they'd suddenly become excellent actors.

They bragged about their fantasies before ordering a pitcher of beer, which spoke volumes.

Chuck had applied for a hunting fantasy in Canada or Alaska. Ralph wanted to experience being extremely wealthy, even if only for a few days. All the answers on Ben's application revealed his wish for hot women, lots of them. Then all eyes turned toward JD.

He sighed, almost certain of how they'd react to his answer. "I want to rest and relax in a peaceful, tropical paradise."

"Boring!" the guys chimed in, shaking their heads.

"Hey, that's what I want, and, win or lose, this better not be a joke."

Each man took one last look at his online application. JD insisted that the phones lay flat on the table in plain sight for all to see. "Ready?" Nods all around. They counted down from ten. With so much volume and drama, other patrons in The Watering Hole joined in the countdown as if the celebrated New Year's Eve ball was about to drop. Upon reaching zero, all four guys tapped their SEND buttons.

JD had given up on being selected, though his friends remained hopeful. He'd gone from thinking the fantasy vacation was a prank or joke to convincing himself the whole thing was a scam or some type of identity theft. That is what he thought until today.

He read the email over and over. Could this be real? He paced, lifted weights, and rode a mile on his stationary bike before returning to his laptop to read it again.

TFM < tfm@tfm.com >
to me
Congratulations! You've been chosen. Your
fantasy will soon come true. A packet will arrive
one week from today. Read it carefully. Be ready
to begin your one-week fantasy on June 20th.
Good times ahead,
TFM

He dashed off to The Casual Gourmet, even though it was his day off. He needed to surround himself with the comforting clatter of pans, the chatter of the kitchen staff, and the aroma of perfectly-cooked food.

"JD, what brings you in today? Want to work an extra shift?"

"No thanks. Just hungry and craving a tri-tip burger." He left out the part about how his head spun with uncertainty and how crazy—or dangerous—his new venture might be.

Later that week, JD returned to his townhouse more exhausted than usual. Three days of double shifts had taken its toll, but after noticing a package taped to his door, his body surged with sudden energy. He rarely received any mail, let alone a package. He hurried inside to take a look.

He found two envelopes. The first one contained a roundtrip airline ticket from Olympia, Washington, to San Francisco and then to the Pohnpei Airport. *I wonder where that is?*

The second envelope contained a short and straight-forward contract requiring his signature. By signing, he agreed that he would not relate the details of his fantasy to anyone. That was doable. He checked both small envelopes and the larger one they'd arrived in, looking for the bill. He wasn't gullible enough to believe this trip was one hundred percent free. The airline ticket alone had to be pricey.

What was the catch? Would he find himself trapped in a never-ending timeshare presentation? Or worse? He wondered what that would be. Did he need to consult a lawyer since a contract was involved? He took another look in the envelopes and found a note the size of a business card. To the empty room, he said, "I knew it was too good to be true." Then he read the words. The note said: "If you have any questions, you may reply by email. TFM."

He had questions. The more he thought about the recent events and communications with TFM, the more unsettled he became. Wanting the night to sleep on it, he went to bed but tossed and turned. Agitated and tired, he got up, opened his laptop, and let his fingers fly across the keys.

JD Middleton < jdcooks@tcg.rinc >
to TFM
What should I bring?
JD

He was shocked when a reply arrived a few seconds later.

TFM < tfm@tfm.com >
to me
Everything you need will be provided, but feel
free to fill a backpack with a few of your favorite
things.
Best of luck,
TFM

He had one more burning question. His fingers moved across the keys, slower this time.

JD Middleton < jdcooks@tcg.rinc >
to TFM
What will this fantasy week cost?
JD

This time the reply didn't come immediately. The Fantasy Maker was likely using a calculator to add up the charges. JD set the laptop on his bed. Wearing only his boxer shorts, he mounted his stationary bike and rode as fast as possible while waiting for the bad news. Wiping the sweat from his muscular body with the towel he kept on the handlebars, he heard the ding announcing the arrival of another email message.

TFM < tfm@tfm.com >
to me
The cost is one week of your time.
TFM

The response baffled him. He had trouble believing there was no charge. Something wasn't right. He thought for a moment before shooting off another question.

JD Middleton < jdcooks@tcg.rinc >
to TFM

What's the catch?
JD

He wondered if his direct question would ruin everything, but he had to know. If there were bad news, he'd rather receive it now than later.

TFM < tfm@tfm.com >
to me
What's the catch? Whatever shows up on the end of your fishing line.
Enjoy!
TFM

Chapter Three

JD

J D arranged to take a few weeks off using some of his accumulated vacation days. He'd finally come to grips with the concept of not working for a while and traveling to an unfamiliar location complements of The Fantasy Maker.

The flight from Olympia to San Francisco was quick and uneventful. His next flight would be long, very long. Standing in line, ready to board the plane, he looked up Pohnpei on his phone to pass the time. Might as well; everyone else stared at their phones. When he discovered the word meant "upon a stone altar," an odd chill ran up his spine, and he put his phone away.

Settled in his first-class seat, and with the take-off complete, JD dozed for a while. Later, looking out the plane's window, he saw a vast body of water, the Pacific

Ocean. He loved the ocean—the color, the scent, the ripples, and the way the sun sank into the watery horizon at the end of the day—but only from a distance.

He'd nearly drowned when he was a small child on vacation with his family. While playing in the shallow water close to the shore, he failed to notice the tide rushing in. A breaking wave knocked him down, pulling him out as it receded. Another wave repeated the first wave's attack whenever he managed to stand. Each time he came up for air, he screamed for his parents to help. Had they not heard his cries?

Finally, after being pushed under the water several times, little JD crawled to the shore, his legs scraped and shaking with exhaustion when he stood on the wet sand. Why hadn't his parents come to help him? Since that terrifying day, he never ventured into any body of water deeper than his knees. Even thinking about that frightening experience made him struggle for air.

As the plane headed toward Pohnpei International Airport, JD created a vision in his mind of a dry, waterless landing. When the plane bumped onto the runway, a feeling of relief swept over him. The directions from TFM had not included information about getting from the airport to his fantasy's exact location. The other passengers that had deplaned with him disappeared quickly. What should he do?

Looking around the small airport, he spotted a man holding a cardboard sign with the letters JD crudely scrawled on it. They both waved. The man shook JD's hand and led him away from the runway to a small seaplane that bobbed up and down at the dock's edge.

"Welcome aboard, Mr. Middleton. Buckle up. Might be a little bumpy 'cause we've got some wind today."

Once in his seat, before the engines growled and sputtered, a wave of a different nature swept over him. Nausea. He must have looked as bad as he felt because the pilot asked, "Are you okay?" He wasn't but was too embarrassed to admit it.

"Flying in these small planes makes some folks feel kind of queasy. Here, have one of these," he said, handing JD a round, yellow pill. "It'll take the edge off, help you relax. This ride will be over before you know it."

Should I swallow this plain yellow pill from a total stranger? Oh, what the heck. It was that, or vomit.

It seemed only a few seconds had passed when JD's sleepy eyes opened. Apparently, they'd landed while he was "relaxing." The seaplane's engine idled, and the pontoons rocked gently on the smooth, blue water. Seeing the beautiful, white sand beach lined with palm trees brought on the peaceful, easy feeling he'd hoped for.

"Wow! The Fantasy Maker really came through."

The pilot gave him a sideways look and a hearty laugh. "That's a good one. Never heard that before."

"Huh. Okay, so what do I do now?" JD asked the pilot.

"Well, you need to get to shore, but this is as far as I can take you. You can swim or take the small inflatable raft I've got on board."

Swimming was not an option. JD would paddle ashore in the raft. Another bout of nausea threatened to make his raft ride miserable.

"Hang on a sec," the pilot said, looking down at the 3x5 card in his hand. "One more little detail. When you do get to shore, go west." Glancing up, he shrugged. "And, FYI— A small cabin cruiser was reported missing yesterday in these waters. I'm guessing those folks just wanted some privacy and didn't want to be found. So don't be shocked if a family shows up here thinking it's a deserted island." The pilot laughed and seemed to find his comment humorous.

After JD was settled in the raft and began to paddle, the pilot revved the engine, skimmed over the water, and soon was no more than a dark speck in the sky.

I can do this. He paddled toward the shore, using his well-developed strength to make his time on the water as brief as possible. With that mission accomplished, he pulled the raft onto the beach, keeping everything dry except his shoes. He made a 360-degree slow-motion spin. Amazing. From where he stood, he saw only calm blue water, a sandy beach, and a tropical jungle. He breathed deeply, enjoying the clean, warm air and stillness surrounding him.

Solitude! No work to do here.

After checking the sun's position, JD followed the

instructions and headed west. As he rounded the curve of the shoreline, he spotted one lone backpack up ahead on the sand. Looking around, seeing no sign of anyone else, he opened the pack and found a note resting on top of its contents that read: "Welcome. You've arrived at your fantasy destination. This is your home for a week, so make the most of it."

JD rummaged through the backpack looking for a snack, but all the pack contained was bottled water and a fishing pole. This was either a mistake, or additional supplies would arrive later. He opened the backpack he'd brought with him. It contained nine items, none of them for human consumption.

He'd packed a swimsuit, a towel, sunglasses, and sunscreen. He'd brought a tropical fish and food cookbook, a small baggie, and a men's fitness magazine. Good stuff. He included his cell phone and iPod but quickly learned neither worked here. Too far from cell service, he guessed. He added his wallet to the pack rounding his possessions to an even ten. Confused and hungry, JD sat on the sand, gazing at the horizon. He needed to think. What should he do first?

He stood intending to search for another backpack or crate of supplies but was distracted by a distant, shadowy, human-shaped vision moving toward him. Maybe, this person had the rest of his supplies and would lead him to a dwelling, a cabana, a hut, anything. As the figure approached, he saw a woman, a smiling, waving woman. Oh, no. Had he checked off the wrong box on his application?

When she was several yards away, JD held up his hand like a crossing guard stopping the oncoming traffic. "That's close enough. What are you doing here?"

Her hands went to her hips. She frowned and countered with, "What are *you* doing here?"

The agreement he'd signed with The Fantasy Maker flashed before him. He couldn't tell her about his fantasy without violating that agreement. "Uh, I'm here to fish and relax, and I wasn't expecting to see anyone else."

Her smile was back. "Oh, okay. Well, want to come to my place?" Damn, she was perky, and he wasn't referring to her breasts. He couldn't even see them because a loose-fitting T-shirt with a big white cartoon cat on the front hid them.

"No thanks. I'll stay out of your way if you stay out of mine."

Still all smiles, she said, "Suit yourself, Mr. Robinson Crusoe." She blew him a kiss and gave him a finger-wiggling wave before turning and walking away.

After their brief verbal exchange, he dismissed the idea of an application error. However, this unexpected predicament annoyed him. And . . . Aw, geez. She wore one of those thong bikini bottoms. He didn't care for that let-it-all-hang-out style on most women, but on this woman, oh, man, did it work. He couldn't take his eyes off her. He'd never seen such a cute, firm butt before.

And those legs? Wow! Last month's centerfold model looked ordinary compared to this gal.

He attempted to remember what her face looked like but couldn't. He blamed his lack of recall on the fact that he'd been trying to ignore her and her presence here in his promised solitude. Just as well. The last thing he wanted was a playful, energetic woman intruding on his peace and quiet.

Summer

Summer felt his eyes following her as she strolled up the beach. She fought the urge to turn around and take another look at him. She'd noticed his sandy-colored hair was much longer than hers and how it rippled like tiny waves when a gentle breeze danced through it. She suspected that a handsome man could be found beneath that serious face. For a guy on vacation, he was darn grumpy. She shook her head and dove into the sea when she caught herself thinking about what he might be hiding under his baggy clothing. There'd be plenty of time for looking later.

The water calmed her. Summer loved to swim, and she was good at it. Not Olympic good, but talented enough to land an added-duty job as the girls' swim team coach. The extra money was essential, but she also enjoyed motivating the girls to do better. Her meager teaching assistant paycheck wasn't enough to make her lifelong dream come true. And with the school canceling classes until September, she set thinking about her future aside. Survival mode took its place.

When Summer reached the lagoon, she got out of the water and walked to her tiny home-away-from-home located halfway between the tree line and the gentle, warm waters of the lagoon. She didn't have much in the way of provisions, but that didn't matter. She'd only be on the island six more days.

Now that she'd seen the man, she decided to tidy up her area. Move the furniture around, so to speak. She'd become lazy over the past few days assuming she was completely alone, but his arrival changed all that. Had her motives changed too?

JD

JD loved food. Creating new recipes, shopping for ingredients, cooking, and tasting his masterpieces was what he lived for. Until today, he'd never experienced gut-wrenching hunger. His stomach growled in protest, demanding food, any food. Confident that he'd find the additional, promised supplies, he wasn't worried about starving to death, but he was damn hungry.

Logic told him to go back and check out the area where he'd been dropped off. That made the most sense. He headed back to the raft with a pack over each shoulder, though something nagged at him to go the other way.

After reaching the raft, he thoroughly searched the

area, expecting provisions from The Fantasy Maker to appear at any moment. Finding nothing, his only choice was to keep walking. After an hour, his fruitless trek left him more confused. Why hadn't he done more research on where his prize would take him? He'd barely checked the destination on the airline ticket. All he knew was his tropical paradise was an island somewhere in the Pacific Ocean. What had he gotten himself into?

As he walked back toward the raft, hunger pangs raging in his mid-section, he thought about the woman. He tried to push away those thoughts because they included visuals of her firm, slender body and her adorable, tousled pixie-like hairstyle. *Good grief. If the guys could hear me now, I'd never live down those words.* But how did she get to the island? Why was she here? She didn't seem to be hungry, so she must have food. Had she taken his supplies and everything that was here for him? That scenario made some sense. *Women!* Still, he'd get to the bottom of this, one way or another.

By the time he reached the raft, the sun was mere inches from the horizon. He chose not to venture deeper into the unknown tonight. Instead, he would take a crack at fishing until the imminent dusk turned to darkness. He sat near the shore connecting the three sections of the fishing rod, attaching the reel, and tying a hook and sinker to the end of the line.

He looked up just in time to see the golden orb disappear into the water, leaving a few rays of light reflecting off a single white cloud. A vision of the woman's recent dive into the water appeared and lingered. He'd still be thinking about her if one critical fact hadn't smacked him in the face. He had no bait. None. Damn!

He drank a bottle of water and fell asleep on the raft. He'd sort out his predicament tomorrow.

Chapter Four

Summer

Summer had always been an early riser, up with the sun and ready to go. Today was no exception. According to her To-Do list, she pulled on her sleeveless, cropped Felix the Cat T-shirt knowing this would be a soak-up-some-sunshine day. Next, she threw several protein bars and a couple of juice bottles into her cloth bag and headed down the beach.

At first, she didn't see her new, grumpy neighbor, but as she drew closer, she spotted him sound asleep in his raft. "Hey, sleepy head. Rise and shine."

He rubbed his eyes, struggling to sit up. "What time is it?"

"Daytime," she teased.

"I'm not an early riser. I work late almost every night."

"You didn't work last night, did you?"

He stood up and rubbed his neck. "No, I guess not, but I didn't get much sleep."

"Want some breakfast?" She handed him a protein bar before he could answer. Without a second's hesitation, he devoured the needed nourishment. "Here. Wash it down with this."

"Apple juice. Thanks."

Did he smile? Actually, smile? Encouraged, Summer invited him to take a walk with her to the other side of the island. He hesitated as if she'd brazenly asked him out on a date. He seemed to be thinking far too much about her simple, straightforward offer.

"Okay, Miss Felix the Cat. My calendar's free, but let's start with introductions. I'm JD. And you are?" She held out her hand and informed him that her name was Summer. Summer Sinclair. "Nice to meet you, Summer. So, do we cut through the trees or go around on the beach?"

"We go around. Too many bugs in the trees—jumping spiders, giant millipedes, and millions of beetles—and though I appreciate all of God's creatures, I don't like the local insects. Except for the raspy cricket. That one's not too bad."

She suggested he wear a swimsuit and bring a towel if he had one. He reached into his pack, pulled out his suit and towel, and surveyed the area as if looking for a dressing room. Summer giggled at his dilemma.

"Turn around," he said.

"You turn around," she countered.

They each turned around, but Summer glanced over her shoulder as he pulled off his khakis and stepped into his suit. She should have looked away but didn't. She'd known he had a handsome face right from the start. The firm set of his jaw combined with his startling steel blue eyes had captured her attention.

But his body? Oh, my. Her eyes froze on his lean, muscular form. He looked good without his clothes. No, he looked great except for his pale white skin. Had he never spent time outdoors? He could sure use some sun.

She hadn't expected nor prepared for such a hot guy to show up on the island. "Ready?" She tossed her empty bag into the raft. "Let's go, then." Summer was determined her beach neighbor would have a good time today, his first full day on the island.

JD

Within moments after they met, JD suspected Summer was a talkative woman. So he was surprised, though grateful, for her silence as they walked. The hypnotic sound of the waves advancing to the shore, lapping gently near his feet, and the occasional cooing of an unidentified bird, were pleasant.

He began to relax, even in the presence of this unwanted woman. He hoped she could shed some light on his missing supplies. If she didn't know where they were, perhaps she had something he could use for bait. With bait, he could catch fish to feed himself.

He was the first to break the silence. "I'm curious, Summer. Why would a pretty woman like you be here on what appears to be an uninhabited island?" She looked displeased. Was it something he'd said?

Before responding, she hesitated as if requiring more time to form her reply. "I'm a middle school biology teaching assistant and a coach for the girls' swim team. Since we're on summer break right now, I decided to take a vacation. You know, a little R & R."

He believed the job portion of her answer, but he wasn't buying the rest of it. There had to be more to her explanation. But what? No pretty young woman would choose to be this far from civilization, alone. What if she wasn't alone? His imagination took a negative turn, but she spoke again before he reached any cynical conclusions. "Well, I'm curious, too. What's a handsome guy like you doing here?"

He had to make something up. Lie. His agreement with The Fantasy Maker did not allow for the truth. He was far from perfect, but he wasn't a liar. This was tough.

"I'm a sous chef, and my friends set up this vacation for me. I have to admit, it's not quite what I expected." There. That was close to the truth.

"You know what? You work too hard."

He came to a sudden halt and felt his face forming a questioning frown. How could she possibly know that?

He's definitely not working too hard here on the island, not yet anyway. Maybe his friends did have something to do with this. Back in Olympia, they often tried to hook him up with a woman. Also, they were the only ones who knew how stressed he was trying to make his way to head chef and, eventually, become the owner of his own high-end restaurant. But, no. That was a ridiculous thought. They didn't have the funds to bankroll a joke this pricey.

Before JD could ask her what she meant, she shouted, "We're almost there," and took off running.

"Almost where?" He ran after her and caught up quickly, although running on sand was a new experience.

Summer

Summer loved the surprised look on his face. She'd been amazed, too, the first time she'd rounded the sudden curve of the land. This picturesque ridge of rocks formed a small cliff and overlooked a dark blue, water-filled cove.

"Come on," she called impatiently. Not waiting for JD, she began her ascent, knowing from experience that the climb wasn't as difficult as it appeared. He could do this easily if he wanted to. His strength and physical fitness were obvious, and he might even enjoy himself, which was her sole purpose for bringing him to this spot.

He arrived at the top mere moments after Summer.

They sat gazing at the view of nothing but blue. Blue water, blue sky . . . and three dolphins! Could this day get any better? No doubt about it, he was smiling now. Not at her, but that was all right. She didn't need his smile for herself.

Summer stood, ready to have some fun. She hoped he'd watch and follow her lead. JD tilted his head to the side to look toward a screeching noise coming from the palm trees to their left. Summer saw him turn back as she jumped from the cliff. Surfacing, she looked around, expecting to see a splash in the water. The splash never came, but within seconds, JD arrived at the cove's edge, wide-eyed and breathless.

"Summer. Are you all right?" he asked, appearing shaken and a little green around the gills. Summer didn't understand why he looked so bewildered. "Yeah, I'm great. Come on in. The water's perfect."

"No. I think you should come out and explain yourself." JD resembled an annoyed shark that had undergone cosmetic dental work.

"What's there to explain? I just cannonballed into the water. I've done it before. I knew the depth of the water, so it was safe. I thought you'd follow me."

"Follow you? I thought you fell off the cliff and might be injured, and then you'd sink and not come up."

"Falling off a cliff and performing a cannonball look nothing alike."

Was Mr. Grumpy showing concern for her well-being? She mellowed, climbed out of the water, and sat with him on the sand. This great-looking guy was hard to figure out, but she'd keep trying.

JD

Though the location sparkled, JD found the limitations and this woman insufferable. He did not utter a single word once they began walking back.

"Do you plan on sleeping in the raft again tonight?" Summer asked, seemingly oblivious to his dark mood.

"I have no plans. I'm still trying to figure out what's going on here."

He had to focus and be careful with his comments, which was easier said than done. He stared out at the water. Her wet, clinging T-shirt messed with his mind. "Okay, here it is. You are correct in your assessment, but I thought there would be more amenities. And I wanted to fish." He paused and turned toward her. "Do you have anything I can use for bait?"

Her cute expression morphed into one of disbelief. "See all that blue stuff out there?" She made a wide sweeping motion with her arm. "You know, the sea? It's a giant bait bucket. You seem like a smart guy. How can you not know that?"

JD's heart began racing. There was no way he would admit he could not bring himself to enter the water deep enough to search for the desired bait, let alone plunge his head under the ocean's surface to see what was there. He'd always been embarrassed by his fear of water, but never as much as today.

Except for his occasional nightmare, he could push that fear out of his thoughts or sweep it under the rug. He avoided participating in water sports. He'd never gone sailing or surfing. Desperate, he thought of explaining his fear to Summer. Maybe then she'd cut him some slack and also some bait. He could do that without violating his contract.

So lost in his own thoughts, he didn't notice her departure. He looked up and down the beach, but there was no sign of her. She must be swimming home. *That is something she would do.*

When he reached the raft, he stared down at his only amenity, his accommodations, his everything. Pitiful. That's what it was. He was never going to find more supplies. Was it possible The Fantasy Maker never intended to fulfill her promise, or was it *his* promise? JD had no idea who had sent him to this island or if Summer had taken the supplies intended for him. He didn't know which scenario troubled him more. Either way, something was definitely wrong. For the second time, he wondered what he'd gotten himself into?

Chapter Five

Summary

Summer unrolled her yoga mat onto the sand at the edge of her cozy island nest. Some of JD's tension had entered her soul, and she needed to regain her joyful frame of mind. With the gentle breeze tickling her short, wispy hair and the sparkling sun warming her damp body, she relied on a few yoga poses to restore her positive energy.

All the stretching and the deep, slow breathing lowered her anxiety. But in the middle of a downward-facing dog pose, an unfamiliar sensation interrupted her meditative state. Guilt? Maybe. Had her attempts to help JD enjoy his vacation become nothing more than selfish manipulation? That wasn't her usual style, and it might be the cause of these sudden, guilty feelings.

Was she trying too hard?

The poor guy had nothing, not even food. A chef without food made no sense. Something must have gone wrong for him. She'd continue with her efforts to show him a good time and keep him from starving because she had a job to do, and she liked him despite his grumpiness. Surprised by that revelation, her meditative state remained elusive.

JD

Letting her in on his fear of water would be humiliating. Admitting that he needed her, depended on her to survive the next few days, pushed and stretched him far beyond his comfort zone. He'd existed within that zone for many years and preferred to remain there.

He could do this, but first, he had to find her. Heading up the beach away from the cliffs and his raft, he watched for any sign of human existence. A footprint, a sandcastle, a protein bar wrapper. Anything. He kept walking, not knowing how large the island was or how far her temporary place was from his. He had no other choice.

JD stopped and was tempted to retreat when he spotted a small white tube in the sand. Upon closer inspection, he determined it to be some kind of lip color with sunscreen in it. It had to be Summer's. He'd seen her applying something to her lips several times. With a legitimate reason to call on her, he placed the tube in his pocket and continued his search.

A slight breeze and the gentle lapping of small waves on the sand helped push aside his anticipated discomfort, allowing him to enjoy this peaceful moment of solitude. A few dragon flies buzzed by, a whitish-gray bird made a dove-like sound, and voices mumbled words. Wait! Voices? He squinted his eyes, trying to find the source of the sound.

Did Summer have company, a traveling companion? She'd never mentioned another person. Or had she? He had to admit he'd ignored much of what she'd said. He saw what resembled a campsite around the island's next curve and moved stealthily toward it.

Nice little setup she's got there.

She had a tent, a real tent, plus a lean-to for shade. There was a fire pit for cooking, a makeshift shelf that held a few pots and utensils, and two coolers that stirred his curiosity. And she was still talking.

"Hi, there," he said, causing her to flinch at the unexpected voice. "Thought I'd stop by if that's all right with you."

"Whoa! You surprised me." She stood and brushed the sand from her hands. "Want something to drink?"

"Sure. Would your friend like to join us?" It made sense that she wouldn't be here alone, but if another human were sharing the island or her tent, he had to know.

"My friend? You're my only friend here." Then she mumbled softly, "Sometimes this guy is too weird." JD heard her words in spite of her feeble attempt to conceal them.

"But I heard you talking with someone."

For some reason, she found his statement hilarious. She giggled, stepped to the side, and with a sweeping Vanna White motion, brought his attention to a plant. A plant.

"So you planted a plant there for the purpose of talking to it?"

"No, silly. I transplanted a plant and then spoke to it. Plants like that, you know." She pointed out several other plants she'd "transplanted" and explained that she wanted a few flowering plants from the jungle close to her campsite. She wasn't about to eat and sleep near the trees, bushes, and bugs.

This woman was beautiful, adorable, and damn confusing. "I could have sworn I heard another voice. I know I did."

"Oh, that was the starling," she answered matter-of-factly as if that were an everyday occurrence. "Where were we? Oh, yes, red or white. What's your pleasure?"

"Red or white what?"

"Kool-Aid," she teased with a hint of sarcasm. "Wine. Red or white?"

He chose red, then watched with astonishment as she reached into one of the coolers and retrieved a bottle of pinot noir. Handing him a corkscrew, she asked JD to open the bottle, then grabbed a couple of wine glasses from the other cooler.

"Wow!" was all he could say as he studied her rustic campsite set halfway between the water and the tree line. Maybe a glass of wine would improve his social skills, and he'd be able to explain the reason he'd made the trip up the beach. One question still nagged at him. Had she helped herself to the supplies that had been left for him?

"Summer, how long have you been here?"

"Hmm. Let me think. Day one was Mickey, followed by Donald. The day you arrived was Hello Kitty Day, and, as you can see, Felix the Cat made his appearance. So I've been here four days. Two more than you."

She poured the wine and handed him a glass. "To a great today and a better tomorrow," she said, looking as happy as a woman vacationing at a luxurious resort.

They sat in silence, sipping their wine and watching the sun sink toward the horizon. He finally admitted he'd had a few hours that he truly enjoyed. Still, he wanted to return to his raft before the sky darkened. He thanked her for sharing the wine, then turned to go. Instead of walking away, he paused. JD had something more to say.

"You know I have nothing, right? Everything I'd need was supposed to be here waiting for me." He stopped short of asking if she'd taken his provisions.

She walked to the cooler and took out two protein bars and another juice box. "Here you go. You really need to get organized and set up a suitable shelter for yourself, or you're going to be redder than a lobster. Sweet dreams." She gave a little finger-wiggling wave—he wondered if that was just her island wave or her usual trademark—and stepped into her tent.

Summer

Summer sat on her sleeping mat in a full lotus position, wondering what to do next. This fun and games beach assignment was not what she'd expected, but she admitted it had sounded too good to be true. She tried recalling the words in the ad and the numerous emails that went back and forth between her and the founder of this travel program.

As she drifted off to sleep, two thoughts came to mind. The fun had not yet begun, and she had no one to play with. Correction. She had an incredibly handsome man she could be swimming, snorkeling or diving for shells with, but he seemed unwilling to play.

Chapter Six

JD

JD woke up hot and hungry. The sun beat down, baking his entire body. Rolling to his side, he reached into his pack and felt for his sunglasses. They were gone. Now he was wide-awake. When he sat up, he saw her. She knelt in the sand near the foot of the raft, twirling his sunglasses in her hand, grinning.

She was as perky as the day they'd met. Instead of Felix the Cat, she was wearing a Pink Panther T-shirt. "Good morning. Looking for these?"

The sun sparkled through her tousled blonde hair creating a golden, aura-like effect. How could a woman look so sexy and angelic and be so annoying? Reaching toward her, he took possession of his sunglasses and then stood up.

"I brought breakfast." She held up a granola bar and a bottle of water.

"Breakfast for one?"

"I already ate."

He devoured the dry, tasteless rectangle she called breakfast and chugged down some water. Grateful for both but sorely disappointed by the meager offering. If only she had something he could cook. He craved a meal with real ingredients, not this pre-packaged, chemically-loaded snack food.

"Let's go snorkeling," she suggested, producing two sets of gear from a cloth bag and holding them up above her head.

"I don't think so. Not today." Something wasn't quite right. "If you're here by yourself, how come you have snorkeling gear for two?" He had her this time. She'd have to divulge what she was up to.

"Unlike you, I came prepared and have back-ups for almost everything."

She answered him so quickly that she was either telling the truth or she'd planned ahead for a question like that.

Seemingly unperturbed by his lack of participation, she tried again. "Why don't we simply go for a swim? No equipment required." Summer was all smiles, looking confident, but he turned down every water-based offer. "This guy is so not a four," she mumbled.

"What did you just say?" Something about her words rang familiar.

40

Instead of repeating her remark, she changed the subject. "What are we waiting for? Why don't you want to have a little beach fun?"

"Because I've got a better idea. Let's go exploring in the trees. We could forage for edibles. Something I could cook."

Summer was as hesitant to walk into the jungle as he was to enter the water.

"On one condition. We have to go back to my place because I am not stepping foot into the trees without shoes. I'll bring a bag or two in case we find something you might want to eat."

Finally, they had a plan.

Summer

After walking a mere twenty paces into the trees, Summer noticed everything felt different. The air held more humidity, the ground more moisture, and sweat formed on her skin. She saw it on JD's too. They were in unfamiliar territory, exploring together, and it felt good to be doing something with a companion. Even so, the further from the beach they traveled, the more cautious she became.

As much as she loved plants and animals, she knew the jungle contained species she'd rather not meet up with. She pointed out a few ground doves and fly catchers, coconut palms and cinnamon trees, and was delighted to find some taro plants. But when she spotted the breadfruit trees, she froze, then went wild, jumping up and down.

JD asked, "What's the matter? Is something wrong?"

She made no attempt to tone down her enthusiasm. "I've only seen pictures of breadfruit trees in books, and there they are, in real life."

"Are they edible?"

"According to my textbooks, yes."

"Have you ever eaten one?"

She shook her head. "Pretty sure my neighborhood grocer doesn't stock them." She picked up the pace, her greenish-gold eyes flashing with excitement.

"According to those textbooks, they're not poisonous, correct?"

"I don't think so. Come on." She took off running toward the group of trees.

When JD caught up with her, she was slamming her body against the tree.

"What are you doing?" he called. "You're going to hurt yourself."

"I'm okay. Just trying to shake down a few of the breadfruits, but if you're willing to climb up the tree, I'll gladly step aside."

She changed tactics and managed to jump high enough to grab one of the tree's lowest branches. "Watch this," she said, prepared to duck from any falling breadfruits she might jar loose. Summer shook the branch, and things fell from the tree. Instead of breadfruit, a multitude of beetles rained down. Hundreds of them crawled over her body, causing her to let out an ear-piercing scream. She swatted frantically at the barrage of insects. Panic set in, and her screams became shrieks.

JD scooped her up in his arms and rushed away from the tree. "Keep your eyes and your mouth closed. Don't talk. You'll be okay."

She followed his suggestions but couldn't keep from hyperventilating and making whimpering sounds. As soon they were far enough from the beetle-filled trees, he set her down and began to brush away the remaining bugs from her skin. The beetles tangled in her short hair had to be plucked out one at a time. The entire experience was terrifying for Summer. Her body trembled long after they returned to the beach, and the bugs disappeared.

His questioning stare was unmistakable. Instead of her usual feisty reaction to almost anything he did or said, tears fell from Summer's eyes. Now, embarrassment trumped the terror she'd felt. He tipped her chin upward and captured her eyes with his. JD's face radiated with kindness as he leaned closer, his lips slowly descending upon hers. Quivering at the unexpected tenderness of his kiss, she melted into his arms.

JD

JD enjoyed the feel of a woman in his arms. No, not just a woman. What he took pleasure in was holding Summer in his arms. The bug incident exposed a vulnerable side he didn't think she possessed. *Should I thank her or the beetles?* As wonderful as their embrace felt, he worried they'd gone beyond her comfort zone. Pulling away, he noticed she was slightly out of breath. "Why don't you take a quick swim?" he suggested. A look of relief flooded her face.

She pulled off her shorts at the water's edge and threw them on the sand. JD couldn't tear his eyes away. After all, he was a guy. Squinting, he focused in on the microscopic amount of fabric that adorned her lower half. Was he staring at a swimsuit bottom or panties? Who cared what she was wearing? He loved looking at that perfect part of her body.

She called back to him, "Why don't you join me?"

"No thanks. I'm fine. I'll wait for you here."

He wasn't fine. If The Fantasy Maker had been more forthcoming about his fantasy location, he wouldn't be here now. This was no place for a man terrified of water deeper than his knees. Three days down, four to go. There was no way he could alter the time frame. Communication with the real world did not exist in his present situation.

Watching Summer walk toward him sent his negative thoughts packing. He focused on her beauty and the splendor of the island.

She smiled and said, "Taking a swim was a good idea. I feel so much better."

"Good enough for a glass of wine and a story?"

She gave him a quizzical look. "A story, huh? Fact or fiction?"

The real Summer was back. He needed to stay on his toes to keep up with this witty, energetic woman. They walked back to her tent site and the coolers. She selected a bottle of red wine, handed it to JD, and then grabbed a couple of glasses. He managed to peer over her shoulder and take a quick inventory of the cooler's contents. It contained some items he'd classify as real food. *I wonder why she doesn't offer me the cheese or the fruit.*

Unexpectedly, she made a suggestion. "Let's go to your place."

"My place? Why? There's nothing there."

She needed no time to invent an answer. She blurted out, "Your raft is there. I'd rather sip wine and listen to stories lounging in your raft. If we stay here, we have to sit cross-legged on the sand. It's a no brainer."

Summer

Summer spread one of her enormous beach towels on the floor of the raft while JD popped the cork. They situated themselves on opposite sides of the raft, allowing eye-to-eye contact. Their backs leaned up against one side, and their feet rested on the other.

Pleased that her raft-sitting suggestion was better than two La-Z-Boy chairs, she raised her glass.

"To us and our stories."

He nodded and chugged the entire glass of wine before stating he didn't know where to begin.

Amused by his comment, she laughed. "How about at the beginning?" She refilled his wine glass and waited.

"It won't be fun to tell. And it won't be entertaining."

Why was he hesitating? *He's definitely a glass-half-empty guy.* Summer guessed the story was not a happy one.

In a single breath, he gulped down the second glass of wine. Frowning, as if he were facing an unpleasant task, he began his story. Looking her straight in the eye, he said, "When I was six years old, I nearly drowned, and I've experienced a mortifying and inconvenient fear of water ever since."

"I'm so sorry," Summer said, moving over to sit next to him. They sat in silence, watching the sun sign off for the day. She threw the extra beach towel over their bare legs hoping that action and the warmth would turn his troubling thoughts into spoken words. When he remained silent, she said softly, "Stories usually contain more than one sentence. Please go on. Help me understand."

He nodded and sighed. "I've never talked to anyone about this before. I kept the fear hidden until I arrived on this beach and met you. Surrounded by so much water makes life here difficult for me."

Once he began to talk, the words tumbled out non-stop. He explained how the waves near the shoreline knocked him down, and every time he tried to get up, another wave was right there to knock him down again. He'd sputtered, coughed, and struggled to breathe.

"Dying by drowning seemed inevitable. Looking back, I thought the waves' strength had lessened or the tide had turned. Either way, I'd been able to crawl out of the water and onto the sand."

Summer attempted to place a positive spin on his life-changing experience. "You survived. It sounds like you saved yourself. That's a good thing. You should feel proud."

"You're right, but there's more. When I had the opportunity and the strength to look up, I saw my parents sitting there on the beach, talking and laughing. Not caring that I was drowning. Apparently, I wasn't worth saving."

No wonder she found JD confusing. He had some serious, long-buried issues to sort through. Issues that needed far more than a vacation to cure. And this was not the best of circumstances for that to take place. Now, she was the one deep in thought, but he kept talking.

"Ever since that day, when I couldn't depend on my parents, I swore I'd never depend on anyone but myself."

"But you're not a child anymore, JD. You can look back with a mature set of eyes and adult reasoning. The water phobia can be overcome." She wasn't that certain about his inability to rely or depend on anyone other than himself.

Chapter Seven

JD

JD opened his eyes to a blinding, bright light. Where had the darkness gone? Had he slept through the entire night? This was a rare and pleasant surprise. He stretched and rolled onto his back. Another surprise! There lay Summer, sleeping like a baby.

As she slept, JD thought about how he would spend his day. First, he'd head back to the breadfruit trees, then explore other jungle cuisine possibilities. After that, he'd gather palm branches and assemble a crude shelter. Yes, day four on the island would be productive. He rose from the raft slowly, careful not to wake her.

By the time he returned with an arm full of fruit, Summer was gone. The two towels were neatly folded in the raft. Was that a sign? A hint? Did she plan to sleep in his raft again? No. She probably swam back to her place. Can't carry towels and swim at the same time.

Proud of his first island accomplishments, JD rewarded himself with some time off. He sat on the sand enjoying the solitude. When the sky darkened, he looked up to see a mountain of clouds billowing above him. No doubt rain was on its way. JD had lived most of his life in the Pacific Northwest, so rain was no big deal. He left the water's edge and retreated to his crude shelter. The approaching weather encouraged him to relax. No running or push-ups until the rainstorm passed by.

Tired, he closed his eyes. His body, having had a taste of a good night's sleep, craved more, but his mind fought that idea. If he slept, his dreaded nightmare might recur as it often did. Instead, he thought about the pretty woman and tried to understand her presence on the island. Why was she so hesitant to explain her situation? She sure was beautiful. And nice and helpful and . . . He dozed off.

A sudden blast of wind and pelting rain wakened him abruptly, quickly becoming the center of his attention. The intensity of this brief storm had ripped his small lean–to apart. At least he hadn't dreamed of drowning. He dreamed of Summer. Was she all right? He needed to know and took off running.

"Hi. Where are you headed in such a hurry?" she asked, apparently unfazed by the weather. She was wet, of course, but that was the norm for her. She spent more time in the water than on the shore.

Seeing she was unharmed and her shelter was in tact, he felt foolish. And the frustration from his recent thoughts and questions about her crept back in. Maybe today he'd persuade her to tell a story or two.

"Just wanted to make sure you were all right. Doesn't look like you had much wind with your rain."

"Nope. But it rained like cats and dogs. Didn't last long, though. The storm arrived early. The rainy season isn't due for another two weeks."

Laughing, he told her, "I must have experienced a micro-burst because my entire shelter has returned to the jungle." Knowing she was safe, his focus returned to unanswered questions. "Speaking of shelters, I'm still wondering how you and all your amenities got here?"

Confused by the question, she glared at him. "You have a problem with my stuff? That I came prepared? That you didn't?" Her tone had become hostile. Where had that cute, perky woman gone?

Fighting the urge to match her tone, he explained. "I'm glad you came prepared but I'm curious. Your set-up doesn't seem possible, plus your being here doesn't make sense. I told you my story and I think you should tell me yours."

Summer frowned. "It's really none of your business. Besides, why do you care?"

"I've got my reasons. The fact that you and I ended up on an uninhabited island at the same time seems more than a coincidence."

Her hands went to her hips. Not a good sign. "Maybe it's fate. Yeah. Ever think of that?"

"Fine. How long does 'fate' intend to keep you here?"

She glared at him, refused to answer his question, and then looked away as if he didn't exist.

Frustrated, JD changed his tone. "For your information, I'm not interested in playing any of your surf and turf games. And, yesterday's kiss was a mistake."

Summer dropped to her knees. "I thought you enjoyed our kiss," she said, as if she were hurt. But, in a matter of seconds, she was back on her feet with hands on her hips and anger on her face.

JD faced the jungle. Summer faced the ocean. They looked daggers at each other in an island standoff, until her demeanor changed, again. Her eyes took on a trance-like, far away look. "Something is out there." She squinted and formed makeshift binoculars with her hands. "What is that?"

JD turned around to see what she was looking at. "Pretty sure it's not a shark. We'd see a fin."

"I agree but, oh, my god! I think it's a dog. And it's struggling."

They shared looks of panic. JD was the first to speak. "We've got to save it."

"You're right. Let's go." Before any discussion of what 'go' would entail, she pulled today's T-shirt over her head, dove into the water, and began swimming toward the animal.

Oh, damn! He stood there, rooted to the sand, for exactly three seconds. Making a decision, he ran back to his raft at record speed. Jumping in, he paddled toward Summer. She'd reached the dog and was supporting it with her arms while her legs treaded water. Together, Summer from the water and JD from the raft, were able to lift the dog to safety. The trembling animal resembled an over-sized, scruffy wet weasel.

"Hop in, Summer. Let's ride back to shore together."

She must have kicked the water with unbelievable force because she popped up like a porpoise and rolled right into the raft. Sitting forward, she held the dog's head in her lap while JD paddled. Would she think less of him because he didn't swim out to help save the dog? Since he'd told her about his water phobia, would she understand his actions? He should have been able to swim in the ocean. He wanted to, but couldn't.

Her voice interrupted his unhappy trip down memory lane. "That was brilliant," she spoke with certainty.

"What was brilliant?"

"Oh, come on. You know. Don't act so humble."

He didn't get it, but hoped she'd explain. Moments of brilliance beyond the boundaries of his duties as a chef were few and far between. No, they were non-existent.

Holding the dog close to her, she smiled, "Going for the raft, silly. That was brilliant. Who knows what might have happened if our only option had been to swim back to shore with the dog in our arms. The current is stronger than usual today."

The strength of the undercurrent became evident to JD when he was unable to steer the raft in a straight line to the shore. The effort to paddle took all of his strength. They wound up closer to his place than hers. The second he beached the raft, Summer jumped out with a splash and pushed the raft further up on the sand. JD stepped out carefully holding the terrified dog in his arms. When he set him down, the dog shook the water from its fur, sharing the dampness with his rescuers, but its body still trembled.

"I'm going home for a quick nap. Why don't you both stop by later for happy hour?"

Evidently, the dog was staying with him. JD didn't mind. Looking up with tired, frightened eyes, the soggy creature tapped JD's leg with its paw. *He's probably thirsty and hungry.* Not having a cup or bowl, JD poured a small amount of water left over from breakfast into his hand. The dog lapped ravenously at the water, much of it spilling onto the sand. Then he threw it all up.

JD waited a while, then tried again. The same thing happened. He hoped the dog was cleansing itself from the salt water it must have taken in during its swim in the ocean. He tried again. Third time's a charm. The water stayed down.

"Hey, buddy. Are you up to coming with me to

gather some palm branches? Maybe we'll find something we can use for your water dish." The exhausted dog stood up and slowly followed, but when they reached the tree line, the poor dog was too tired to continue. "Okay. Wait there. I've got to rebuild my shelter this afternoon or Summer will give me a hard time. And take it from me, you don't want to be around for that."

There. That should do it. He stood back and admired his work. The structure was an improvement over his first attempt, though that wasn't saying much. Looking skyward, he estimated the sun would set in two hours.

"Let's go. We don't want to keep the lady waiting." JD began the trek up the beach hoping the dog would follow. The dog, still lethargic, stood for a moment, then returned to a sitting position. As tired as he was, he came up with the energy to whine, magnificently.

Shrugging, JD picked up his new furry friend and carried him all the way to Summer's place.

Summer

Seeing them approach, joy bubbled up inside her and she smiled. "Hi guys. You're just in time." She'd set out two low beach chairs. JD sat in one, and the dog sat next to him, ignoring the towel she'd placed between the chairs.

"Today you have beach chairs? Since when do sporting goods stores deliver to uninhabited islands?" He shook his head and raised an eyebrow.

"You're too funny," she said, making light of his comment.

She tried to imagine what it must be like to be so confused about a simple, straightforward vacation, though she didn't understand why a good-looking guy like JD would choose a remote island. Then again, he wasn't much of a people person. What troubled her more was why he acted shocked, almost angry that she was here.

Summer wished she hadn't signed that contract with Vacations Unlimited requiring her silence, practically a gag order. She'd agreed not to discuss the details of her temporary assignment with anyone, no matter what happened. She hadn't given it much thought at the time, but now she, too, desired some clarity, some understanding of the situation.

"I keep the chairs in the tent. Care for some cheese with your wine?"

He laughed. "That's a good one. You're all right, Summer."

Ah. A positive comment from her guest. He liked her wine.

"The dog looks much better with its fur dry and fluffy, don't you think?"

"You know, according to science, this dog has hair, not fur."

He just looked at her, shook his head, and refrained from making a comment.

They established the dog's gender and agreed that he needed a name. Each time one of them had an idea, Summer wrote it in the sand using a piece of a large shell as a pen. Dog, Waterdog, Swimmer, White Dog, Buddy, Flipper, but nothing sounded like a good name for *this* dog.

"What kind of a dog do you think he is?" Summer looked curiously at their new companion. "I've never seen one like him."

"Not sure. He must be a mixed breed. He's got the size and shape of a Border Collie, but his wiry, oatmeal-colored fur is unusual."

The dog struggled to stand, then walked stiffly to the tree line where he peed. Would he keep walking and enter the jungle? He looked back over his shoulder as if wondering what he should do.

Was the dog simply tired? Summer hoped he wasn't injured or sick. JD made the choice for the indecisive dog. He walked over, picked him up, and carried him back. For that, he got a kiss. A kiss from the dog.

"He seems to like you. What's your secret?"

"Dog biscuits."

"What? You have no human food but you have dog treats?" She found that amusing. Giggling, she asked, "Why?"

"One never knows when they might be in the company of a dog."

Summer squinted her eyes and tilted her head. "Nope. Try again. I'm not buying that story."

JD laughed, enjoying her confusion. "Okay, if you insist. In the seat pocket in front of me on the plane, there was a plastic bag containing dog biscuits. I don't know why I took them with me. Before I ran into you, I was so hungry I considered eating them myself. Got any cat cookies? You seem like a cat person to me." He pointed at her T-shirt.

"Oh, that. I have dog shirts too."

"Good to know. Now, the important question is do you have any food a dog could eat? I'm out of biscuits and he's probably starving."

That presented a problem. The dog lacked food. Neither of them thought the limited fruit and vegetable choices on the island would be good for him. He needed protein.

"Let's check out your coolers. There must be something in there he could eat."

Other than several packages of Ramen, Hamburger Helper minus any meat, and more cheese, everything else was snack food.

"This is what you eat?"

"No, well, yes. This is what I eat on the island because I don't cook. Back home I eat out or call in an order for home delivery. I eat healthy food."

"Well, you're not eating healthy here. And that's going to change right now. You need protein. We all need protein. Where can a guy get crabs around here?"

Had he meant to be funny? She hoped so because she laughed so hard she needed to visit the tree line.

Ignoring the insinuation, he said, "Hurry up, water-woman. You're catching our dinner before the sun goes down."

"Hang on. I need to grab a knife."

He took her hand and they dashed toward the water. "What's the plan?"

She led him further west to a rocky area with several tide pools. "It would help if we had a net, but since we don't, our best option is to gather a few abalones. They hang out on the rocks. It would be easier to get one if the tide were lower, but I think I can pry one loose for tonight's dinner. Just remember, I've never done this before, so no laughing."

It seemed their nameless dog didn't want to be left behind. He began his slow trek toward them as Summer entered the water.

She tugged and pried at the iridescent shell, forcing it loose from the rock, and then tossed it onto the sand. It was small so she collected two more.

"There you go. I did my part. Now you get to do yours."

The dog never made it all the way to their abalone-gathering site. JD picked him up and carried him back. Summer took charge of their catch.

She'd never eaten abalone, let alone cooked it. From the expression on JD's face, she wasn't so sure he had either.

"I know what your thinking, Summer. Rest assured, I have cooked similar sea snails before, but they arrived in butcher paper, not shells."

For the fun of it, he rattled off a minimal list of his food preparation needs. A frying pan, a very sharp knife or strong spatula, peanut oil, and panko bread crumbs. She produced a frying pan, a not-very-sharp knife, and a stick of butter. That was the best she could do.

Happy to be occupied with something he did well, JD smiled and began to build a cooking fire with the driftwood piled behind the tent. He looked up at Summer. "For a woman who doesn't cook, I'm pleasantly surprised you brought a frying pan and butter."

Summer shrugged. "I didn't pack that stuff, someone else did. I packed clothing, my sleeping mat and lip gloss with sunscreen."

"Someone else packed for you? Are you a spoiled rich girl?"

"Very funny." She hadn't meant to divulge that someone else was involved and wished she could take back her words.

Summer rummaged around in one of the coolers and held up several packages of ramen. "How about this for a side dish?"

"Looks good. Got another pot for heating some water?"

She brought JD a pot, sat down next to the dog, and watched the chef go to work. JD had a tough time getting the abalone meat from their shells. When the reddish-beige blobs of the delicacy were finally free, he cut away much of the outer layers before slicing what was left into thin strips.

"Is JD a nickname?"

"I guess you could say that."

Summer wished she had his talent for being evasive. Not letting him off the hook, she continued questioning him.

"What's your given name? You'd better tell me or I'll start guessing."

"JD is short for Jeffery Dylan, but don't you dare call me that."

"I won't." *Hmm. Jeffrey. Jeff. Chef Jeff.* She liked that. "But I might call you Chef Jeff when you're preparing food."

He shook a finger at her and silently formed the word, no, before turning back to the frying pan. The butter sizzled with the addition of each slice of abalone. *Frying makes anything taste good.* The abalone smelled delicious.

"So, now you're a fish chef."

Focused on the cooking, he admonished her. "The correct term, *poissonnier*, sounds so much better."

She rolled her eyes. "I'm not so sure about that."

The abalone and the ramen satisfied their hunger. Combined with pleasant conversation and the dog, they enjoyed a perfect evening. The after dinner clean-up felt like the cherry on top of a delicious dessert. JD's arm brushed against hers several times, and once he'd placed his hands on the bare skin at her waist to move her to the side. All perfectly normal, ordinary actions, no big deal, but her heart beat rapidly and her skin tingled.

They watched the golden sun slip below the horizon before saying goodnight. JD and the dog headed down the beach. Summer watched, waved until they were out of sight, and wondered what tomorrow would bring.

Chapter Eight

Summer

U p with the sun, Summer sang to the sky, to the plants, and to all the creatures in the sea as she prepared a special breakfast. Special, considering her lack of cooking experience. Fortunately, for Chef Jeff and the dog, there'd been leftovers from the night before.

Instead of heating the abalone and chicken flavored ramen in two separate pots, she mixed them together and a crumbled up granola bar to give it texture, a little bit of crunch. Voila! Her first casserole.

Am I trying to impress the chef?

That didn't matter. She'd impressed herself. She pulled a Scooby Doo T-shirt, long enough to be called a cover-up, over her swimsuit, grabbed the pot of food, and walked swiftly down the beach. When she rounded the curve of the shoreline and the raft came into view, she saw the floppy tips of the dog's ears before his whole head pop up over the side. *Hmm. Someone doesn't like to sleep alone.*

Standing beside the raft, she watched the dog lick the sleeping man's face. He mumbled words that sounded like, "Love you too."

"Good morning, sleepy head. Time to get up. Breakfast is served!"

Summer lifted the pot filled with breakfast encouraging JD and the dog to rise and shine. The dog jumped out first.

They both stared in amazement at the dog's display of energy. He smiled, wagged his crooked tail, and then trotted over to the trees to pee. He sniffed around before trotting back to his people. His nose led him straight to the food-filled pot. Summer and JD laughed, watching him dance with excitement. Breakfast time had arrived.

Summer took three abalone shells from the pot, the island's version of fine china. Filled one for the dog, then another for JD.

"This is good, really good, Miss Pretends-Not-To-Cook. See, two can play your name game."

She dished up a small serving for herself. She liked it, but the dog? He loved it. "He seems especially fond of the noodles. Noodles. We could name him Noodles."

JD shook his head. "We could, but let's think about that while you tell me a story. It's your turn."

She knew it was, still she hesitated. He'd wanted to

hear the story of why and how she ended up on the island. She wanted to tell him, but couldn't.

"I can see you need a story-telling prompt. How about this? Once upon a time there was a young woman named Summer and her lifelong dream was ..."

"... to learn all about plants and someday open up her own flower shop. There you go. How was that?"

"Excellent start! Keep going."

"There's not much more to tell except that my dream takes money, a lot of money. My teaching job doesn't provide enough funds to finance my business venture. I can barely support myself."

"When the money train, or the millionaire, or a winning lottery ticket shows up, will Summer, the florist, be married or single?"

"That's kind of personal."

He nodded. "Yes, it is. So was nearly drowning and being afraid of water."

Realizing JD was right, she sighed and began her broken-hearted story. She'd had three boyfriends that she'd cared deeply about. The first one came along during her senior year in high school. She was in love, but he was just horny. Love number two showed up when she attended California State University. She'd spent most of her free time completing his class assignments. He disappeared the day summer break began.

Summer felt tears forming in her eyes and tried to blink them away. JD took her hand. She loved the way her skin tingled whenever it came in contact with his.

"You can stop anytime. It wasn't my intention to make you sad. I just want to know more about you."

"That's okay. I've been selfish, and you need to know why I'm not going to fall in love with you."

JD let go of her hand and leaned back. "Hey, I have no intention of falling in love, either. Remember, I came for peace, quiet, and solitude." He paused to take a breath. "By the way, someday I plan to open my own high-end restaurant. That also takes lots of money. See? We have something in common."

"Let me finish, please."

She continued. During her first year of teaching, she'd met a man working on his PhD, or so he'd said. He was good to her. They had fun, until she stopped paying for some of his expenses. Bottom line, they all broke her heart.

"I only want to play on the beach, when I'm not in the water, and enjoy my time here. I have no intention of leaving this island with a broken heart."

Summer stood, looked deeply into his intense blue eyes, then turned and walked away.

JD called out, "Hey Scooby. When are you leaving the island?"

Her walk broke into a run.

JD

Already noon and he'd accomplished only one thing. He'd upset Summer, his lifeline. Without her water, her junk food, her beautiful self, he'd be in bad shape. She'd kept him alive. *Am I using her like those other guys did?*

He'd never asked her for anything; she'd volunteered everything. She was a sweet, kind, lovable woman most of the time. There were moments when he'd been blindsided by her tenderness. He liked everything about her except for the way she closely guarded her secrets. His curiosity about her overwhelmed him, but he couldn't deny the existence of his own secrets.

Sitting in his rebuilt crude shelter with the dog in his lap, he flipped the pages of the cookbook he'd brought. It contained plenty of promising fish recipes. If only he had the necessary spices and some fish. But what was the point? He was leaving the day after tomorrow.

JD was a guy of action, and that was part of the point. This much down time didn't serve him well and his body trembled from inactivity. If he were back in Olympia, he'd work off his excess energy in his home gym or create a new recipe in his kitchen. And going into work was always an option. But here? Damn! What he wouldn't give for a no-whip café mocha right now.

Pushups. Running on the beach. Crunches. That was about it. He acknowledged that the dog was a good distraction and fun to be with.

Noticing the warm weight had left his lap, JD put the book down, stood up and spotted the dog walking along the tree line. "Where you going, buddy?" The dog looked back at JD as if beckoning him to follow.

Apparently, he'd detected an interesting scent or wanted to see Summer. JD wanted to see her too. Being at odds with his island partner didn't feel right. Whatever her secrets, her quirks, her issues, he could be her friend for a couple more days.

JD let the dog set the pace. Though the pace was slow, he didn't act as if he wanted to be carried this time. He took a slight detour into the trees and stopped next to a patch of beautiful flowers. JD didn't know if he was more amazed by the flowers or by the dog's ability to locate them.

They found Summer sitting on a beach chair a few feet from the water's edge. She stared trance-like out into the ocean as if she were hypnotized. The ocean usually produced a smile on her face. Not today. Was that his fault?

To gain her attention, he and the dog stepped into her line of sight. He held out the flowers. "A peace offering from me and Noodles."

Her faint smile morphed quickly into an ecstatic, wide-eyed expression of joy. He'd hoped the flowers would please her, and it seems they did.

"Sederia japonica! Oh, my gosh! They're beautiful. Where did you find them?"

"Noodles gets all the credit. He discovered them."

Holding the flowers in one hand, she rubbed the dog's head with the other. "Sounds like we're going to call him Noodles." JD was touched by her excitement over a bunch of flowers. He wanted to hug her but held back. "Unless you want to call him sedrajep, that word you just said."

"That word is the name of this orchid. Even though I've never owned one, it's at the top of my list of favorites. They're grown mostly in Japan. Did you notice its lemony scent? Isn't that the best?"

"Yeah, they do smell good. You know a lot about flowers, huh?"

"Of course. My dream is to be a florist. Run my own shop. Didn't I mention that?"

Nodding, and then he confessed that heading to her place was Noodles' idea. "I would have come over eventually because I felt an apology was necessary." Upsetting her was unnecessary. He hadn't meant to make her sad or angry.

Setting the orchids on the chair, she flung her arms around his neck. "Shut up and kiss me."

Wow! Flower power. Amazing.

One joyful kiss. What harm could come from that? He held her beautiful face in his lemon-scented hands and brushed a gentle kiss across her forehead. Hearing her encouraging sigh, he kissed the pulsing hollow at the base of her throat, then wrapped his arms around her, pulling her close. Her soft, slender curves molded into the contours of his lean, muscular body. It was the feel of her nearly naked back that reawakened a long-forgotten need. *Oh, geez. I should stop.*

When her sighs intensified, his body responded. Any thought of stopping disappeared. He moved his mouth over hers, devouring its softness. There was a dreamy intimacy to the kiss. Had she felt it too? Later, he wondered where that delicious kiss would have led had Noodles not barked when he did. Their romantic moment was gone in a flash.

Summer laughed. He loved it when she laughed. "Look what the tide brought in."

Noodles and three large crabs were in a standoff. They were taking turns chasing each other. First the crabs charged at the dog, then he herded them away from the water. This back and forth game of chase went on for quite a while until Summer and JD stumbled upon the same revelation at the exact same moment.

"Dinner!"

Now it was three on three, but those crabs were fast. In the end, there remained one crab and two slightly injured humans. Summer, not wanting to pick up a fast moving crustacean, had retreated to her fire pit and returned with the biggest pot she could find. While Noodles and JD endured crab claw assaults, she trapped one under the pot.

"I got one!"

Taking his focus from the task at hand, JD's intended catch ran away and Noodles chased his into the water. Tonight's main entrée would consist of three small servings of the delicacy. That was better than nothing.

They filled the crab's temporary home with seawater and covered it with a lid. Then placed a good-size piece of driftwood on top, in case it had thoughts of escaping. Summer tenderly rubbed the claw marks on JD's hand with an antibiotic cream on the chance that his skin had been punctured. Noodles licked his left paw, taking care of himself.

"I've got a question for you, but you must promise not to get mad."

Still attending to his hand, she replied, "You can ask, but I can't promise. I'll try to keep an open mind, though."

"How much water do you have left?"

"There is another cooler full under that tarp over there. You thought that would make me mad?"

JD blew out a long breath. "I'm not finished. This is a two-part question. I liked your answer to the first part."

"Uh, huh. Go on."

"I want you to know my vacation is over day after tomorrow. How much longer do you plan to stay?"

Instead of answering him, a frown crossed her face and she raced to the ocean and walked in up to her calves. She stomped and kicked at the water as if that were her enemy. JD watched curiously, disturbed by her reaction to such a simple question. Her assault of the sea went on for at least five minutes.

"Here she comes, Noodles. Act normal, don't say anything," he whispered to the dog .

She strolled past them to the cooler and poured two glasses of white wine before returning.

"Cheers!" She took a sip, then another. "I will spend at least two more days on the island, maybe four, maybe five. I'm not sure yet." JD was about to speak, but she wagged a finger near his face. "And that's all you're getting from me."

"Okay, but I have more for you."

That went better than he'd expected, though the uncharacteristic aloof look on her face hinted at deceit. He'd return to that topic later. They remained silent, sipping the wine until their glasses were empty. JD broke the silence. He told her they needed more nutritious food for the three of them to get through the next two days. She'd need more if she stayed longer. "I think we should spend the rest of the day searching for food in the jungle."

"No. Absolutely not. I will not go back in there."

"Hear me out. It's going to be okay, really. Do you have a long-sleeved shirt?" She nodded affirmatively. "How about long pants?" She said she had some lightweight yoga pants. "I know you have shoes. How about a floppy hat?" Another nod. "Then we're good to go. I won't let anything hurt you, but you must promise not to shake any trees or bushes. Go change."

He packed water, extra bags, and utensils that would help with any cutting or digging they might do. When she stepped out from the tent, it was all he could to keep from laughing.

"What are you looking at?" She sounded annoyed. He needed a good answer.

"I'm looking at you, babe. And you're looking very, how shall I put it, safe."

She glared at him, but he detected a twinkle hidden within that glare and a hint of a smile on her face.

Noodles followed. He'd accepted them as his pack, his family. His presence brought out the best in them. Today, they felt secure in each other's company.

Summer came to a sudden halt before entering the humid, darker environment.

"You, Mr. Jungle Boy, must promise me something.

"Okay."

"Since I agreed to go food foraging with you into an area you know terrifies me, not to mention the recent, horrible beetle brawl, you must agree to go fish foraging with me tomorrow. I won't let anything hurt you. Deal?"

JD's stomach lurched. Damn. She drove a hard bargain.

Chapter Nine

Summer

Summer lay happy and content on her sleeping mat, her smile so bright it seemed to light up the tent. What a difference the past twenty-four hours had made. She considered the food foraging expedition a huge success. One of her coolers now housed several breadfruits, taro roots and leaves, and even a couple of coconuts.

The experience had lessened her wariness of the jungle. Not one bug had assaulted her the entire time. Who could have predicted they'd make such a magnificent team? A team of three. Once they'd found the first taro plant and dug it up, Noodles took the lead. He'd dash ahead, locate another, and begin digging.

The earlier crab hunt resulted in one of the best dinners she'd ever eaten. Chef Jeff—that's what she called him when he was cooking, even though he wasn't fond of the nickname— had outdone himself. He'd built a fine fire, boiled the water, and tossed in the weary crustacean. Prior to the toss, they'd graciously thanked him for his sacrifice. The only regret? There'd been just one.

The best part came later. She had a sleeping companion for the entire night. Stroking his back, she snuggled up closer to Noodles. JD had insisted he stay with her. In a great mood, he declared they had joint custody of the dog, and it was her turn to keep him.

"Rise and shine, puppy dog. Our dog-daddy will be here soon."

Time passed with no sign of JD. Did he intend to renege on his promise? She wouldn't be surprised, as she understood his phobia. But after eating several meals of delicious seafood, her palette and her stomach hungered for more.

She carried two chairs and the empty pot down to the water's edge. While waiting for JD to arrive, she and Noodles shared a granola bar and watched for a crab.

"Hi Summer, Noodles. Sleep well?"

"As a matter of fact, we did." She produced another granola bar for JD. "You're late. We thought you might not show up."

"I had things to do. Being a no-show crossed my mind. Just for the record, I think this is a bad idea. But I keep my promises."

The vulnerable look on his face was easy to read.

Her heart ached for him and the fear he felt. She'd be gentle and they'd go slowly into the water.

"What are you looking at?" he asked.

She wanted to repeat the line he'd used on her yesterday, but those weren't the words that tumbled out. "I'm looking at a man who's wishing for some floaties. Can you swim?"

He answered, "Sure." But she didn't believe him.

"I learned how to swim before the ocean tried to take me down. It's just like riding a bike, right? Once you learn, you never forget."

She was grateful for his positive approach to what was about to occur. He wouldn't need to swim this morning. They would wade in thigh-high water, about eighteen inches beyond his comfort zone, to gather one or two abalones. She preferred crab, and there were other fish in the sea she'd love to try, but today their catch would consist of abalone.

"Follow me. Check your footing and the water depth as you go."

The tide was higher today and soon they were up to their elbows in seawater. JD looked tense, so she stayed by his side. After prying two abalones from the rocks, Summer suggested they take them to the cooler. Relief was written all over his face.

"That's not much food," he commented, looking down into the cooler.

She grabbed two pair of goggles and his hand. "Oh, we're not done yet," she said coyly as she tugged him back to the water. "Besides, you were great, so we might as well continue with the water lesson."

Her professional swim coach attitude surfaced, and she explained the next lesson as if speaking to her swim team students. "Here. Put these on. We're going to walk out together and simply take a look under water. Let's see if there is anything out there we might want to catch. Still got your fishing pole?"

"Yeah, but I wish it was an upside-down periscope. And, if you're going to keep barking orders at me, you ought to be wearing a John Madden T-shirt."

His sense of humor was alive and well. So was hers. Face to face, they held hands and practiced holding their breath. When she was satisfied he was ready, she guided him downward until their heads were covered with water. Submerged for only a couple of seconds, Summer gave a thumbs up and they rose back to the surface. JD gasped as if he'd been without air for hours.

"Great! That wasn't so bad, was it?"

They repeated this drill, each time adding a few more seconds. After the fourth dip below the water's surface, which lasted eight seconds, JD said he was done. He'd honored his promise. "Just one more. A three-second dip. Then we'll stop. Really."

"What's the catch?"

"Well, it's not a snapper, though I think I saw some swimming around. I want you to kiss me beneath the water. Please. Humor me. And don't forget to hold your breath. Ready? Dive." She pulled him under.

The kiss started out better than okay, but was cut short when he popped up coughing, sputtering.

Summer made light of his discomfort. "You know, that would have worked perfectly if we hadn't laughed."

"I wasn't laughing." JD's fists were clenched as he walked to the dry sand.

Nothing was funny now. She congratulated JD for his courage, but he didn't act as if he'd heard her. She tried to place herself in his shoes, but couldn't. Her attempt to help him had backfired. Big time.

The coughing and the hovering tension had a negative effect on Noodles. With his tail between his legs, he slinked around as if he'd done something wrong.

Not ready to give up, Summer suggested, "Sit down and give your dog a hug. He needs you. I'll be right back with drinks and snacks for all of us."

Summer returned with one abalone shell filled with water, one bottle of water, one bottle of wine, and two glasses. The dog eagerly lapped water from his dish. JD reached for the wine glass, but was handed the bottled water.

"Rinse that salty taste out first."

He nodded. "Good idea."

With everyone sitting and drinks all around, she produced two small packages of chips. Real, store-bought chips. Shocked, JD asked, "Why have you been holding out on us? Got any more of these?"

She didn't. She'd saved the snack from the first leg of her flight here.

"And just where is 'here'? I'd really like to know."

"I don't think we're supposed to know where we are."

"We? You'd better start talking. What the hell is going on here? I need to know."

"Well, that makes two of us." She ran into her tent wishing it had a door she could slam.

JD

JD stomped toward his raft. Noodles followed him, but stopped half way between the tent and the raft. He would not budge.

"Suit yourself. But, just so you know, your dinner at the raft will be far better than your dinner by the tent."

He stared down at his treasure trove of jungle treats piled in the raft. This being his last night on the island, he'd risen at dawn to secretly gather enough food for a special date-night dinner. Surprisingly, he'd found some bananas. Dessert! In spite of their disagreements, he'd planned the special dinner to show Summer how grateful he was for all her help. He wanted to leave on friendly terms, and give her a kiss goodbye. Now, his plans for a romantic evening had disintegrated and he'd likely be eating alone unless Noodles joined him.

The torment of the water fiasco convinced him to revert back to being a loner. For the first time in his life, he lost his appetite and had no interest in cooking. Instead of a rumbling stomach, his mind grumbled with anger. He kicked at the sand, threw pieces of shells into the water, and fast-pitched a coconut at the trunk of a nearby tree. The damn thing not only rolled back to him but, son-of-a-gun, the nut had cracked.

The crack was small, but if he found something he could wedge into it, he might be able to whip up a banana-coconut treat. Summer would love that.

His anger and frustration pushed to the side for the moment, he grabbed the taro root and fruit-filled raft's rope, tugged it into the water just far enough to make it float. He was able to pull the raft in Summer's direction without too much trouble.

Noodles was sitting in the same spot, but came trotting over when he saw JD.

"You want a ride?"

The dog leaped up and over the side, then sat up straight in the front part of the raft, resembling a hood ornament.

JD laughed at the dog's antics. "I'll take that as a yes."

Towing the raft, the fruit, and the dog through the small, lapping waves was slow going. Walking on the sand would have been faster than trudging at the shore, but then he wouldn't have been able to bring all the goods. The raft contained dinner, plus extra food for Summer in case she stayed several days longer.

He spotted her over by the tide pools with the big pot in hand. "Hey, Summer!"

She looked up, dropped the pot, and came charging at him.

"Oh, shit," he mumbled quietly. Was she still mad?

As she drew closer, he knew she'd been crying, so he hurried toward her, met her halfway.

"What's the matter? What happened?"

"I thought I'd never see you again."

"Isn't that what you wanted?"

"No. Well, yes. Not exactly." She sniffed and wiped her eyes. "I wanted you to like me, but you were always angry."

"I'm not angry with—Look!" He pointed out that a crab had hopped out of her pot.

"Ugh!" She went after it. JD and Noodles watched, though the dog acted anxious to join in the chase.

"Okay. Let's go lend a hand."

That crab zigzagged sideways dodging its three attackers who blocked its path to the ocean. The minute it stood its ground a little too long, Summer slammed the pot down, capturing the crustacean a second time. The dog barked, JD applauded, and Summer took a bow.

"Tonight we dine on crab legs, mashed taro root, fried breadfruit and—a drum roll please—banana-coconut pudding."

Summer cheered and performed a silly happy dance at the mention of the menu. Then she leaped at him, throwing her arms around his neck and wrapping her legs around his waist. He'd never seen her so happy.

Still wrapped together with Summer's breath tickling his neck, JD said, "It seems the power of food is out-performing flower power. Good to know because I'm good at food." Laughing, and feeling light-hearted, JD explained, "This may take a while, so let's get cooking." Back at her campsite, he began peeling and chopping the taro root. He stopped to glance at Summer. "Without any spices, I make no guarantees."

After hearing his expression of doubt, Summer ran into her tent. Was it something he'd said? When she came back out, he saw right away that she'd exchanged her Baloo T-shirt for a short, silky sarong. Grinning like a Cheshire cat, she held out a plastic container like one of the Three Wise Men bearing a gift. A cartoon version of Pandora's Box flashed through JD's brain. He shook his head to clear away that image. He never knew what to expect when it came to this woman's words or actions.

"Here, try these." A proud smile lit up her face as she handed over the box.

"Spices? You know this makes absolutely no sense, right? You've told me several times that you don't cook."

"That's right. I don't." With her arms spread wide, she glanced from left to right. "Somehow, this box got packed along with everything else."

He'd heard that explanation before, but wisely, he made no comment and turned back to his food prep tasks. He focused on the fact that the spices would greatly improve the flavor of the food. But he wondered what else she had in her tent and where it had come from if she had not brought it herself.

Summer

The meal was to die for. Chef Jeff had outdone himself. Even Noodles ate everything except the mashed taro root. Summer cleaned the pots and the abalone shell dishes, then opened the last bottle of wine. JD set the chairs near the water. Facing the western horizon provided a magnificent view of the setting sun. Neither spoke.

A melancholy feeling swept over Summer. She wondered what JD was thinking. He appeared relaxed, his wine glass in one hand, petting Noodles with the other. What would become of Noodles? This was their last night together. She felt awkward bringing up the topic of the dog, but time was running out. Had JD considered the dog's future? There the adorable dog sat, content to be with them, panting, his tail wagging, not a care in the world.

As if he'd read her mind, JD asked, "Do you ever wonder where Noodles came from?"

She replied immediately. "No. He's a gift from God."

"I do recall the pilot who dropped me off here mentioning that a boat had gone missing the day before. I wonder if Noodles had been on that boat."

"What if the boat sank, and he was the only survivor?"

"In that case, I'll go with your first comment on this subject."

84

"But what if he jumped or fell from the boat? And his owners were still looking for him." Summer wished that theory had not come to mind.

"We could investigate that possibility if we ever return to civilization."

"You mean 'when' we return."

"Of course."

It was important to Summer that JD leave the island happy, thinking he'd had a good time in spite of their difficulties. She couldn't deny that the dog played a major role in JD's fun. He seemed more attached to the dog than he was to her. Was he aware of the dog's dire situation? She tried to imagine a happy ending for all three of them. Her attempts failed.

The fate of the dog had to be decided. "You could take Noodles to a dog shelter when you get back," she said, her voice soft with genuine concern. "He's such a great dog. He'd be adopted right away."

JD nodded, but didn't speak.

Summer assumed the worst. "Yeah, I suppose getting him back to civilization would be difficult."

His curt response came back. "I can't do it."

Summer was confused. Not that she needed to understand what he'd meant by *it*, though that would be nice, but she wanted him to leave happy, no matter what. Or this odd island experience would have been for nothing.

"Do you mean you can't get him on a plane?"

"No. I can't leave Noodles here all alone. He needs us. He wouldn't survive."

His comment not only surprised Summer, it pleased her. "We need him too."

Finally, they agreed on something. And now she had no doubt he had a heart, at least for the dog.

"Would you stay with me tonight? Since your raft is already here, you might as well. It makes sense."

JD said nothing, so in her mind that was a yes. She pulled the raft closer to the tent and proceeded to transform it into a bed using her two pillows and the large beach towels.

"Want to take a short stroll on the beach before we turn in?"

JD stood up and took her hand. "Yes, I'd like that."

They walked in silence with Noodles at their side and the newly risen moon illuminating their way.

JD cleared his throat. "Will you accept my apology for being such a jerk when we first met, pushing you away every chance I got? This whole setting caught me off guard. It wasn't what I expected. Then you came along, all beautiful and energetic."

"Why did you keep pushing me away?" Summer asked. His actions didn't match his words.

He paused before answering her question. "Because you kept coming at me. You were relentless."

Summer hadn't needed him to like her, that wasn't part of anyone's plan. But she needed him to enjoy his vacation, and if he'd decided to like her, so much the better.

"I hadn't requested a woman, not even a companion. The idea of a relationship hadn't entered my mind. I'd requested solitude." He looked up and down the beach, into the jungle, and out at the vast body of water. "That aspect of my fantasy vacation may have been taken too literally."

His statements did not add up. She knew her face held a serious frown and was grateful that a recent gathering of clouds lessened the light of the moon. He really hadn't expected someone like her to be here. His presence was no surprise to her. He was the one and only reason she'd been sent to the island.

"Of course, I accept your apology. You're a good man, JD. Obviously, Vacations Unlimited screwed up somewhere along the line. But let's make the most of this last night. Deal?"

He reached out and shook her hand. "Deal!"

Somewhere between stepping into the raft and falling asleep, they snuggled up like spoons. Three spoons. Feeling safe and childlike lying between a strong, muscular man and a lovable dog, she relaxed, enjoying this final night together on the island. It wasn't long before the sensations brought on by the skin-to-skin contact with JD overpowered her innocent, warm-fuzzy feelings.

Lying in the raft was similar to sleeping on a waterbed. When she rolled over, the bed also rolled. As a result, Noodles scooted to the far end of the raft. Sweetly stroking JD's face, prickly from six days without a shave, he responded with a sleepy moan and traveling hands that sensually stroked her calves, then her thighs, settling even higher, taking her breath away.

He took the top position, hovering over her, kissing her nose, her eyelids, her ears as gently as a whisper. When his lips reached hers, they were persuasive and too powerful to resist. He wasn't like the other men from her past that had broken her heart. JD was different. Certain that sex and love were one and the same with this man, she gave herself permission to go with the flow, ride the wave of passion.

Catching his breath, he pulled away. "I can't do this. My life has no room for love or sex right now."

Frustrated, hurt, and angry, she said, "I'm not asking you for either." Not wanting him to see her cry, she jumped from the raft, hurried toward the water, and struck an angry pose.

JD ran after her. "I don't want you to be sad. I'm trying very hard not to hurt you," He grabbed her arm, but she pulled away, refusing to look at him. "You're a beautiful, wonderful woman. Someday you'll find someone to love and cherish you." He looked around. "But not here."

She'd been wrong again, but found the strength to look him squarely in the eye. "You don't get it, do you?"

"No. I guess I don't." His tone heavy with frustration.

Flustered, she shouted, "I am only here for the money."

Shocked, he looked at her. "You expected me to pay you for your time here with me?"

"Ugh! No. How could you think that? The company paid me."

JD shook his head and punched the air. He had no reply.

They sat on the sand in silence for what felt like an eternity. Summer wanted to say something, shout something, but she couldn't come up with the words.

Taking a deep, calming breath, JD said, "Let's turn back the clock. We can't end our island experience like this."

His words diminished her anger. "What do you have in mind?"

"How about a goodbye kiss followed by a good night's rest in the raft?"

She didn't speak, but took his hand and led him back to their island bed.

Chapter Ten

JD

JD awoke to a sky filled with dark, ominous clouds. Without a visual on the sun, it was impossible to know the time. He stepped from the raft quietly, not wanting to wake Summer. He couldn't bear to say goodbye to her a second time. *What is it about a goodbye kiss that makes you want to stay?* Last night their goodnight kiss and their goodbye kiss had been one and the same. From the look on her face, JD knew how sad she was.

Noodles looked up at him, his head tilted to one side. He gave the dog one last scratch behind his ears and whispered, "Stay. She'll take better care of you than I ever could." Then, sadly, he headed down the beach to wait for his ride home.

Assuming he'd be picked up at approximately the

same spot he'd been dropped off, he sat on the beach with his nearly empty backpack. He'd carry home his useless devices, his book and magazine, his swimsuit, and the unused fishing pole he'd been provided.

What weighed heavy on him were his mixed emotions. Now that it was time to leave, part of him didn't want to go. In less than a week, having Summer as his island neighbor had been a game-changer. She added much to his life in spite of his resistance to her efforts. He didn't completely understand why she bothered with him. Now that he'd be leaving, he told himself it no longer mattered.

Tomorrow he'd be back in his apartment, running on the treadmill, anticipating his return to work. His raison d'être. His everything. Why wasn't he ecstatic at the thought of returning to his normal routine? He closed his eyes and tried to focus on his real life, his dream of owning his own restaurant, becoming one of the world's celebrated chefs, but his thoughts drifted back to Summer. Summer and Noodles.

He could envision their smiling faces, hear her laughter and the dog's joyful bark. Wait. He did hear that. Opening his eyes, there she stood all decked out in a new T-shirt. Apparently, today was Wonder Woman Day.

"Hi. Mind if we wait with you? It could be a while, you know."

"Sure. Suit yourself." He tried to keep an even keel and not look as happy as he suddenly felt. It wouldn't be fair to encourage her. Starting today, they would each go their separate ways.

"Who's coming for you?" she asked.

"I don't know. I wasn't given that information. I wasn't given any information. I guess another seaplane will land out there and . . . Damn!" he said, huffing out a frustrated sigh. "I need the raft."

"Why?"

"Because the seaplane can't land on the beach. I'll need to paddle out to deeper water to catch my ride."

Their conversation was cut short by a drastic change in the weather. The ocean breeze became a howling gale. The moist air turned to rain. Noodles cowered between them for protection, his body trembling.

"I don't think your seaplane will land anywhere for a while." She shouted. "Let's go wait it out in my tent."

He could barely hear her words, but got the main idea. The three took off running. The brutal winds came from the west making their forward progress difficult and slow. They stopped midway, exhausted, out of breath. The rain no longer fell as drops, but poured as if from buckets. Visibility was nearly zero. The beach all but disappeared. They struggled through knee-high water where the sand should have been. Noodles dashed for the trees.

"There goes my tent!" Summer yelled, watching it tumble over and over before going airborne like a lopsided kite, quickly out of sight.

Then it hit. Not a wave, but a wall. A wall of water. "Summer, run into the trees and grab onto . . . "

The surge knocked JD down. He tried to stand, get his footing. The depth of the water wasn't over his head, but its force wouldn't let him up. His head went under and his mind traveled backwards. Back to when he was a six-year-old boy being pounded by the surf. Once again, no one would rescue him. Had he come full circle? Had the ocean come back to finish him off twenty years later?

No! He wasn't that kid anymore. He was a man. A strong man. He struggled, reaching through the dark, fast-moving water to get a grip on something, anything. His shirt caught on a branch, slowing him down, pulling him under. Sputtering, coughing, he came up to see Noodles float by and then slam into the trunk of a nearby palm tree. He couldn't tell if the dog was dead or alive.

"Noodles!" he shouted.

The water carried the limp dog further. Without thinking, JD went after him. Going with the flow of the water rather than fighting it, he reached Noodles within a few seconds. Grabbing the dog by the scruff of its neck, he kept him from being washed away again. Once he managed to lift Noodles into his arms, he held the dog tightly to his chest, then wrapped his own leg around a branch of a breadfruit tree and waited, hoping he could hold on until the overflowing ocean water receded.

What seemed like an eternity was likely less than fifteen minutes, but Summer was on his mind the entire time. When the water level lowered enough to expose his kneecaps and the surge lessened, then retreated, he began his search for Summer. He didn't know where his sudden strength came from, but there it was. Even carrying Noodles, he felt stronger than ever.

Summer

Lifting her sore, aching head from the sand, Summer squinted at her surroundings. Nothing looked familiar. Where was she? Rewinding her memory, she recalled the wind, the rain, and her tent flying through the air above the waves. A sudden rush of water had swept her off her feet, and then engulfed her. She wouldn't call it swimming. The encounter had been more like tumbling, wrestling with the fast-moving water.

Her powers of recall took her no farther. She raised herself up to a sitting position for a better look around. That slight movement instigated a wave of nausea. Along with feeling queasy, she realized she had no strength. None at all.

The wind and rain had stopped. Where were Noodles and JD? How were they? She needed to find them. Again, she looked around but her vision blurred. Everything had a reddish tint. Everything. Even the water that surrounded the small piece of land she'd washed up on.

I'm on a tiny island? No. That can't be.

She franticly wiped her eyes trying to clear her vision. That helped, but her hands were red with blood. Frantic, she felt her head and found cuts dripping blood into her eyes and down the side of her face. Examining herself, she discovered numerous cuts all over her body. Suddenly, they began to sting. A mean Mother Nature had rubbed salt into her wounds.

Re-evaluating her physical condition, she was thankful that the cuts, though messy, were minor. At least she wouldn't bleed to death, but being trapped on this tiny island posed a serious problem. Thinking of the absurdity of the situation, she giggled as she imagined herself as a cartoon character, washed ashore on an elevated patch of sand with one lone coconut palm in the middle, and she was the one desolate human leaning against it. The giggle gone, she forced herself to get serious and make a plan.

She had to figure out where she was and then find JD and Noodles. Holding on to the coconut palm for support, she was able to stand and take a good look in every direction. With a sigh of relief, she saw behind her a much larger island that had to be *their* island.

The island wasn't far away, but the distance across a body of water was a challenge to calculate with any accuracy. There was also the fact she hadn't an ounce of strength. Her fingers and toes were shriveled like pale, skinny prunes, partly from being wet for so long and partly from dehydration. She needed to wait until she regained her strength. *How do I get stronger without food or water?*

More annoyed than scared, she sat down, leaned against the coconut palm, and stared at the only thing there was to look at—their island.

She must have dozed off. When she awoke, the sun was low on the horizon and would soon be out of sight. Panic set in. Remaining on this tiny island all night long sent chills up her scratched and battered spine. Her mouth felt like it was filled with cotton balls. Was she going to starve or die from lack of liquid? Or drown if the tide covered this pile of sand she now sat on?

What she saw next made her entire body shiver and shake. Was it a mirage? A heavenly vision? Did she have a traumatic brain injury or sunstroke? Was this a hallucination? No matter what she called it, JD and Noodles were walking on water toward her. She had to be delusional.

"JD?" She asked, her voice quavering.

He waved. "None other. We've been searching for you for hours."

She wanted to run to them, but not only was she too weak to move, she didn't have the necessary walking-on-water talent in her toolbox. Tense with anticipation, she watched as they moved closer, not trusting the reality of her vision.

The man, resembling a young Robinson Crusoe

with dirty, matted hair touching his shoulders, and the dog, looking soggy and pitiful, stood where the water met the sand.

"Permission to come aboard, ma'am?" JD asked, a weak smile forming on his face.

"Permission granted!"

JD pulled her up a standing position and held her close to him. Noodles ran around them, wagging his tail and barking. This was no mirage. They'd all survived in spite of Mother Nature's untimely wrath.

"We should get back while there's still some light," JD said, pulling away from her and brushing the sand from her cheeks.

"Yes, let's go home. But how did you get here?"

"If you meant our island when you said home, yes, we'll go there, but don't expect it to look homey. Everything is gone. Getting there is easy, though. A sandbar connects the two islands. We can walk on it, if we hurry. The tide's low and the water's only about a foot deep."

Within fifteen minutes they were cutting through the jungle gathering breadfruits that were on the damp ground. Exhausted, they each took a few bites of the raw fruit, then curled up on the sand in each other's arms, confident that either her ride home or JD's would show up tomorrow.

Chapter Eleven

Summary

Summer

Sitting up slowly, stiffly, Summer sighed. JD had been right. Everything was gone, and now their beach, strewn with kelp, fallen palm fronds, and a few dead fish and birds, resembled an odd junkyard. Still, she acknowledged the miracle. They'd all survived the storm, the flood.

Noodles whimpered in his sleep as his legs pretended to run, or were they swimming? A doggie dream for sure. She patted his head and gently rubbed her hands all over his body checking for injuries. He lifted his head, then rolled onto his back for a belly rub. He'd recover but needed fresh water. They all did.

Not yet awake, JD mumbled, "Are we there yet?"

Running her fingers through his messy, sand-filled

hair, Summer replied to his sleepy ramblings. "I don't think so. Where are we going?"

"The boat."

There she sat between two dreamers. "We're going to a boat? What kind of boat?"

He groaned. "The love boat."

A man dream for sure. She left them sleeping to get up and assess their situation. She didn't have the strength to go far. When she reached the ocean's edge, she stared down at the calm, sparkling water. An uneasy feeling crept over her. She had no desire to step in, not even with her toes. She'd always loved oceans, rivers, lakes, and even backyard pools. Shaken by her feelings, she backed away from the water's edge and smack into JD.

He wrapped his nicked-up arms around her and whispered in her ear. "Today's a new day. And the way I see it, we have only three tasks ahead of us. We'll build a simple, palm branch shelter on the beach, we'll search for fresh water, and then we'll wait."

She pulled away to face him. "No matter whose ride shows up first, and no matter what type of transportation it turns out to be, all three of us will leave together."

Continuing to talk, they agreed a misunderstanding must have occurred. Perhaps they were to spend seven full days on the island and get picked up on the eighth. Or the storm delayed yesterday's pickup. Either way, today was the day they'd return to civilization.

"Hey, Summer. How come you'd said you might

remain here longer than me? Now it seems you were expecting us to depart on the same day."

He didn't sound angry, just confused. She hated lying to him, but what choice did she have? She remained unwilling to fail at her job. If she answered his question truthfully, she could lose everything. Being exposed to their near deadly experience would have been all for nothing.

"I did say that, didn't I? Don't know what I was thinking." To change the subject, she quickly said, "I know where we can find fresh water."

The life-saving news distracted JD from his questioning. "Great! What are we waiting for?"

Summer led the way past the tide pools and further west into uncharted territory for JD. She stopped long before they'd reached the far end of the island.

"If you cut through the jungle, there's supposed to be a spring about one hundred yards straight in."

When he asked how she knew about that water source, she replied, "Go. Just go."

"Come with me. We should stick together."

"I have no shoes, no pants. I can't do it."

"You did it yesterday."

"I must have been delirious then. I'm not now."

"I'm shocked," he said, his twinkling eyes contradicting his words. "You're still wearing my favorite shirt. So come on, Wonder Woman. Let's go find that water."

She didn't enjoy the walk and cringed often, but they found a natural spring. The small spring trickled from a rock formation similar but smaller than the one she'd jumped from at the opposite end of the island. The falling water formed a pool where it landed. Noodles began to lap at the water immediately, but Summer pulled him away.

"There might be salt water in the pool that would make us sick or dehydrated more than we already are. We'd better drink directly from the miniature waterfall."

JD guided the dog's mouth to the fresh water. He caught on right away. The humans took far longer to quench their thirsts. They remained near the fresh water for over an hour, taking drinks often, and hoping they'd be picked up before they needed more.

"Do you want to set up a temporary shelter at your old place or mine?"

Summer thought for a minute. "I think we should set up somewhere new. As long as we stay on this side of the island, I'm sure we'll be found."

In a way, Noodles gave them the idea for the new, short-term location—halfway between their former island homes. That made perfect, logistical sense. They needed only some shade where they could rest and recuperate today while they waited for the transportation that would take them home.

Their simple shelter was set up and ready in about thirty minutes. All three prepared to relax until their ride arrived. By the time the sun had moved only an inch across the sky, JD said, "I'm tired, banged up, but I can't just lie here doing nothing."

"I'm so glad you said that. I can't either."

"What do you want to do?"

Summer thought for a moment and said, "Games. Let's play games. We can start with tic-tac-toe." She ran to the jungle's edge and returned with a stick, four stones, and four shells.

"We're really going to do this, huh?"

He watched as she drew the lines for the game in the sand.

"Do you want to be stones or shells?"

JD took too long to answer, so Summer said, "I'll be shells. You're stones."

They played for a while until Noodles got involved and their game board became a hole in the sand.

"Thank God for dogs," Summer said, sounding relieved.

"Amen," JD answered, laughing. "We need something that all three of us could do together?"

"Catch or keep away."

"We'd need a ball."

"I know, and I can make one. I'll be right back."

Again, Summer ran to the jungle and brought back two handfuls of leaves. Within minutes, she dunked the leaves into the sea, scrunched them up into a tight green ball, and tossed it to Noodles. He caught it mid-air and brought it to JD. Game on!

"Here you go, little buddy."

The game of catch was fun. The dog made sure JD and Summer had several turns at tossing the ball. He even decided when the fun and games needed to end by lying in the shade of the shelter. Summer joined him followed by JD. Time to rest.

JD

JD awoke to the sound of Noodles' excited bark. Still half asleep, he looked toward the romping dog and spied the reason for all the barking. "It's only a crab." Wait. What the hell? Something wasn't right. Had he fallen asleep? Their plan was to relax, rest, while they waited for their transportation to arrive.

The sky was gray, though no clouds were visible. The sun must have dipped below the horizon, and they were still waiting. He nudged Summer.

"Hey, babe. No one's come for us and it's almost dark."

She sat up and studied the sky. "It's worse than that." She pointed toward the east. "It's almost light. Day eight came and went, and we're still here."

"That shoots down our theories."

Something had gone terribly wrong.

They sat in silence, each hoping to comprehend their situation.

Was JD stunned more by his overwhelming fear for their survival or the sudden passion he felt for Summer? Both left him in a bewildering state. She might not want that kind of attention from him after her three unsuccessful tries at love. Did he use the word love? Really? He hadn't been looking for romance, but he hadn't wished to be stranded on a deserted island either. Survival before passion. For now, he'd go with that thought. He must.

"Want to hear my plan?" He tried to sound genuinely upbeat, though that wasn't his nature in the best of circumstances.

She nodded, appearing foggy and definitely not her usual, positive self.

"Finding or making something that will hold water is our number one priority. We can't walk back to the spring every time we need a drink. What do you say?"

Her mood changed, the fog lifted a little. Her throat hoarse, she said, "If you bring me several palm fronds I'll weave baskets while you search for food and anything that will help us get a fire started."

JD shouted to Noodles who was occupied close to the shore. "Come on, Noodles. We have work to do." The dog watched the crab crawl clumsily into the water, then trotted back carrying his new treasure between his teeth. One large crab leg.

Summer

Summer, the swim team coach, had no desire to submerge herself into the sea. None at all. Since the flood, the vast amount of blue frightened her. She felt small and helpless. JD, on the other hand, seemed to have evolved from Mr. Grumpy, Mr. Glass-half-empty, to a take-charge, positive attitude island guy. Was he faking it for her benefit?

Doing nothing didn't sit well with her. What could she do if not swim? Annoyed with her current mental state, she struck a few yoga positions. That helped until thoughts of karma crept in during the lotus pose. What had she done in her past to deserve such a negative payback? Nothing significant came to mind.

Had taking this job, doing something merely for financial gain, set their unfortunate situation in motion? She hoped not.

If Noodles hadn't begun to lick her face, she'd likely be sobbing. But there he was with JD close behind. He'd brought the palm fronds and a few breadfruits and said that was all he could carry, but he'd go back for more. At least she had a project to keep her busy for a while.

"Hey, are you okay? Should I stay with you?"

"No, I'll be fine. Just thinking too much, you know?"

He sat beside her, leaned closer, then kissed her eyelids, and nibbled her earlobes. "Think about that while I hunt for bananas." He ran back into the jungle, but this time the dog stayed with her.

Her attempt at transforming palm fronds into baskets proved complicated. The first one looked more like a small, green planet made by a young child than a basket. Attempt number two resembled a basket, but not one that would hold water. The third time was, indeed, a charm. Voila! A basket was born. She was so pleased with herself that she laughed out loud.

She kept the second basket because it could hold something. She crumpled up her first attempt and pitched it into the sea. Noodles jumped in after it likely thinking it was a ball. She smiled at his playfulness. He'd come a long way since the day they'd met.

"Noodles," she called. "Come back, you're getting out too far. Noodles, come!"

The dog tried to return but the current was too strong for him. He kept drifting in an easterly direction, further from the shore. Petrified, Summer kept calling as she paced the water's edge. She cupped her hands to form a megaphone and screamed as loud as she could.

"Noodles, come back. You can do it. You must." She was paralyzed, unable to dive in after him. Had their time with this wonderful dog come full-circle? Would the current carry him to others that would rescue him? Or a fate far worse?

"I'm coming. Hang on, buddy."

Before she realized what was happening, JD rushed past her and ran down the beach parallel with the dog. A lot of good that would do. As she watched, he surprised her by diving into the water. How was a man who panicked when his face went under water going to swim in the ocean? What was he thinking?

Shocked and speechless at first, Summer soon became the one running down the beach, calling for Noodles and JD. He hadn't been swimming since he was six years old. Swimming in a strong ocean current was not for beginners, not even muscular ones. Between Noodles' dog-paddling and his meager weight, he'd be caught up in the current for a long time. She couldn't bear the thought of life without them.

Both of their heads were still above water, a good sign. Gaining back some of her strength, she was determined to make it a threesome in the deep blue sea. She had a strategy. Once she got ahead of them, she'd speed swim toward them at an angle so they would be close enough to grab one another. They'd sink or swim. And they'd do it together.

Putting her newly acquired aversion for seawater aside, she dove in and swam like hell hoping to catch up. When she finally paused and looked in every direction for JD and the dog, all she saw was choppy blue water.

Scared to death that they'd drowned, she swam in circles. Swimming out deeper, she swam to the far eastern end of the island. No wonderful man, no lovable dog in sight. They were gone, and she'd be gone, too, if she didn't get her weak body up on dry land.

JD

"What are you doing way down here? We've been looking all over for you." Two sets of eyes hovered above her. One set appeared worried, the other darn happy.

"I thought the sea had swallowed you both. But you

didn't drown, you're here. We're all together again." She cried so hard her shoulders shook.

JD pulled her onto his lap and held her trembling body. He didn't know what else to do. Had his sudden dive into the ocean alarmed her? Heck. He'd shocked and frightened himself with that move. *Good thing swimming and bike riding have something in common. Once you learn, you never forget.*

Noodles put a halt to her crying when he dropped his green ball in her lap. "How did you manage to save this? Or, rather, *why* did you save it?"

"It wasn't me. That was all his doing."

"Oh, dear. Then he's got a belly full of salt water." As soon as the words left her mouth, the dog began to vomit.

"Wait here." JD sprinted all the way to the spring, picking up her woven water carrier on the way. The dog was in dire need of fresh water.

Upon JD's return, Noodles took small drinks of water but wasn't up to walking. Was his second battle with the ocean too much for him? JD carried him back, and Summer talked softly to the dog and gently patted his head.

Exhausted from the heavy doses of mental and physical stress the day had cast their way, they ate raw breadfruits and bananas, drank water, and curled up together on the sand. Though, no longer waiting for their ride home, JD hoped and prayed for some kind of rescue.

Chapter Twelve

Summer

"The sun will come out tomorrow," Summer sang, surrounded by a mass of green kelp.

"Good morning. What makes you so happy today?"

"Net-making. See? I've figured out how to weave the kelp together. With a net, we should be able to catch fish."

The prospect of a fish dinner excited them. Being practical, JD said, "First, we need to build a shelter even more substantial than your original campsite."

There he goes again. Raining on my parade. "No. That's not necessary. Someone will come for us." Her cup half-full attitude was in rare form today. "All I need is a little food and water to tide me over until I go home."

"Be reasonable, Summer; face reality. We don't know what tomorrow will bring. Could be a ride home, another storm, or something completely unexpected."

Their differing opinions about island survival techniques and how they should spend their time escalated into a full-blown argument.

"Fine. You do it your way, and I'll do it mine." She stomped up the beach about one hundred yards where she sat for the rest of the day. What bothered her the most was the stress it put on Noodles. Once again, the poor dog sat halfway between her and JD.

As darkness approached, it occurred to her that she had neither food nor water, but she wasn't about to head into the jungle by herself, especially this late in the day. The anger she'd felt that morning had vanished hours ago, but her stubbornness kept her from returning. Would her attitude betray her, put them all in danger? What if JD was right and they needed to prepare for the worst?

Swallowing her pride, she walked down the beach toward JD. To her pleasant surprise, he was walking toward her, dragging the net behind him. They met in the middle where Noodles greeted them, his crooked tail making energetic, lop-sided circles in the air. They embraced and simultaneously said, "I'm sorry." They kissed and remained in each other's arms until Noodles decided the net was his new toy. A brief tug-of-war ensued. JD won.

"Your net works well. See?"

He showed her the three fish he'd caught. Their joy diminished quickly, though. How would they cook JD's catch? They had no way to start a fire and were certain no steel or flint would be found on the island. Neither were desperate enough to eat raw fish today.

"We could dry them in the sun tomorrow. That might work." She searched his serious eyes for a flicker of agreement or a speck of hope.

He dropped the net and encircled her with his newly tanned, sand-covered arms. "Yes, we'll try that, but tonight, I'm afraid we're still on the banana and water diet."

For them, that was better than nothing, though Noodles, needing more, added a few insects to his diet.

They sat in the darkness discussing JD's suggestion of creating a new campsite. Summer admitted it was a decent idea and would give them something to do while they waited for help. Now that her mind was open to that venture, another thought snuck in. One that terrified her.

"Hey, girl. What's the matter? You're gripping my hand with such force, it hurts."

"Oh, sorry." She trembled despite the air's warm temperature.

"Sorry? That's it? Talk to me."

She let out a long heavy sigh. "What if no one comes for us?"

He freed his trapped hand from her clutches and placed his arm around her. Frowning, he released a troubled sigh. "I'm surprised that you thought of that possibility. It crossed my mind too."

Their brainstorming efforts began, but in a completely new direction. They hypothesized theories for the lack of transportation. Maybe someone wished them harm. Did either of them have enemies? They didn't think so. Perhaps this was nothing more than a miscommunication regarding the duration of their stay. That was their best hope, though highly unlikely.

Summer brightened, "I'll bet our entire adventure is part of a survival show and we are secretly being taped."

"Interesting. What should we do about that?"

Without the slightest hesitation, she snapped her fingers and sang. "Let's give them something to talk about." Her mood lifted at the mere thought of her wild and crazy idea, and she giggled. At times, Summer could be playful even in the midst of dangerous uncertainty. What harm could come from a little levity and a good imagination?

JD

Was his island companion teasing? Just playing around? Or did she mean business? So far neither had made a move. Instead, they intently studied each other's expressions. JD concluded that she held a look of anticipation on her face. He encountered his own version of anticipation, but it didn't come in the form of a look and it wasn't on his face.

Before he could take her hand or hold her in his arms, she was on his lap with her legs wrapped around his waist, running her fingers through his hair.

"I guess we really are giving *them* something to talk about."

Her hands grasped the bottom of his plain T-shirt and lifted it over his head. "Yes, we are. And we've only just begun." She looked around, waving at imaginary cameras. JD loved this impish side of her. The girl was a player.

This was a game he'd enjoy. But first, he'd level the playing field. "Wonder Woman has got to go," his tone serious as he removed her T-shirt. He expected to see a scanty swimsuit top, but instead, he found himself gazing at her sweet, perky breasts. Chest to breasts, skin on skin, had they reached the point of no return? He hoped no cameras were rolling.

His thoughts messed with his performance. While Summer nibbled his neck, he rationalized his long-practiced modus operandi of avoiding any relationships with women due to his future career plans. Did he even deserve a woman, especially one as wonderful as Summer? That bothered him more. He desperately wanted to outrun his useless thoughts, leave them behind. *Stop thinking!*

He got his wish. His body took over, his career thoughts set aside. He felt the heat, the arousal. Gently, he repositioned Summer's lovely female form from his lap to the sand. Lying on her back, her green eyes sparkled in the moonlight, tugging at his emotions. Gazing down at her slim, fit body, it was as if he'd just seen her, really seen her, for the very first time. She was beautiful, athletic, smart, and damn sexy.

He wanted her, all of her. Closing his eyes, thoughts didn't get in the way this time, but a strange, ridiculous vision did. An annoying robot waved its arms around and shouted, "Warning! Warning!" Where had that come from? Was it an omen of things to come?

Summer's hands coaxing the shorts from his hips sent that vision packing. JD stood to facilitate the complete removal of his clothing. His desire for her had no place to hide. He reached for her hand and helped her up, then knelt down and guided the thong-style swimsuit bottom to her ankles. Naked, they embraced under the shimmering light of the moon.

She moaned and whispered in his ear, "What took you so long?"

He had no verbal reply. Instead, his mouth covered hers again, taking her lips in an eddy of deep, sensual kisses. A hot tide of passion raged through them until the watery tide of the ocean cooled their feet and everything else. JD cradled her in his arms and carried her beyond the incoming tide's reach. Noodles bounded to the dry sand with them. Apparently, he'd been ignored long enough and needed their attention. The threesome sat on the beach, enjoying the beauty of the moon and the soft, hypnotic sound of the lapping waves.

"Another theory just occurred to me. Maybe my

helicopter went down in the storm. Now that makes sense."

"You own a helicopter?" That didn't make sense.

"Oh, it's not mine. That was the transportation provided by Vacations Unlimited."

"You must have paid a large sum of money for your vacation if it included dropping you off in a helicopter."

When she didn't reply, JD's frustration mounted. More mysteries, more questionable information. No matter how attracted he was to her, he wanted answers. He needed the truth.

He positioned his body directly in front of her so they sat knees to knees. "I have a few things to say. It's possible your transportation could have been grounded or lost in the storm. But the fact that both of our rides home failed to show up is much tougher to believe."

He took her hands in his and gazed earnestly into her eyes. "Tomorrow, we will lay down every damn card we're holding and every shred of information regarding our island circumstances. The whole truth, nothing but the truth, will be shared, set out in plain sight. No more secrets. Okay?"

She nodded, snuggled up with Noodles, and drifted off to sleep with a smile on her face.

JD had too much to think about. He lay sleepless on the sand for hours.

Summer

Summer awoke first, overflowing with high energy and good spirits in spite of being stranded on a deserted island in the middle of nowhere. She focused on the positive, lived in the moment, and felt certain today would be the day their ship would come in. Not literally, though, since she was expecting a helicopter.

Squinting into the recently risen morning sun, she saw an object wash up onto the shore. No, there were several objects. Running to the water's edge, she recognized one rubber container as her own. Upon opening it, she could not hold back her excitement. Gifts from the ocean. This was better than Christmas.

"JD, hurry. Come see. You'll be able to cook again."

That got his attention, though he moved slowly.

In one hand, she held a long-nosed lighter. In the other, a small pan. Not a frying or a crab catching pan, but a pan they could use for cooking.

"Is that your backpack?" She pointed at the beat-up old pack lying on the sand.

"No, it's not." Cautiously, he struggled with the zipper. What could be inside?

A new look spread across Summer's face that included wiggling eyebrows. "Let's guess."

"You do like to transform the most mundane things into fun and games. Go ahead and guess. You've got until I manage to get this inoperable zipper to work."

He kept tugging until he forced it open. One by one, he removed the items. There were several zip locked plastic bags containing rotten remnants of someone's lunch. A shriveled up apple, a waterlogged, unidentifiable paperback book, and a knife.

"The knife might come in handy, but the rest—"

Undaunted, Summer said, "We will find a use for everything. Maybe not the apple, if it really is an apple."

They agreed that the backpack, even in its deplorable condition, could be used to carry items from the jungle to their crude campsite. The pages of the book, once dry, would be kindling for a fire. Driftwood gathering would take place later in the day.

"I'm making a trip to the spring to refill our water bag. You want to come?" Only Noodles showed an interest in taking the long walk. Summer declined, more interested in watching the sea for additional gifts it might offer.

JD

JD returned with the day's water supply, then set to work whipping up a smoothie consisting of bananas, water, and a few mashed up pieces of the unidentified fruit. They renamed the drink a *chunkie,* since instead of going down smoothly, it required chewing.

Their moment of truth could not be put off any longer. And so it began. Taking alternating turns, each would ask one question of the other. "Ladies first." JD insisted.

"Why did you choose this island for your vacation?"

"Coming to this location was not my idea. The

Fantasy Maker created the trip for me. All I'd requested was peace and quiet in a tropical setting. I don't know the name of this island or if it even has one. I don't know where it's located. I assume we are somewhere in the Pacific."

Before speaking, Summer's hands found their way to her hips, and a frown formed on her pretty face. "Hmm. I thought we were supposed to be telling the truth. You're asking me to believe that someone you call The Fantasy Maker sent you here? Who is that?"

He thought for a second, then answered, "The creator of my fantasy vacation, but now you've asked three questions. It's my turn. You've mentioned Vacations Unlimited several times. Tell me about that organization."

She shrugged. "They hired me to keep you entertained for one week."

"You're getting paid to entertain me?" He had surmised she was making money for her time on the island, but not like this. "Just how entertaining were you supposed to be?"

He felt the heat of anger building up inside of him. How could these words she spoke be true? Again, nothing she said made sense.

"Definitely not what you're thinking. My contract required that I keep you company, take part in a little beach fun, and call if either of us had any problems."

"Call? How? None of my techie stuff works here."

She sighed and looked upset. The relationship they'd begun to build was rapidly deteriorating.

"It was a satellite phone. And like everything else, we lost it in the flood."

Shaking his head, JD said, "So you expected me to be here, while I was completely shocked by your presence. I don't understand how or why that could have happened."

"I don't either, but I wasn't allowed to talk to you or anyone about this arrangement. If I did, I would not only take a cut in the agreed upon pay, but I'd lose the bonus."

The part about not being able to discuss the terms of the contract had a familiar ring, but he didn't like the sound of payments and bonuses. JD did the best he could to explain how he became involved with The Fantasy Maker.

"Me and three of my best friends answered an ad one of their girlfriends had seen in a magazine. It said something like Wanted: a few good men. We were to call a number and leave our email addresses. We did that and filled out our applications when they arrived. Several weeks later, I received a notice that I had won a fantasy vacation. From the beginning, I was leery and thought it was a prank or worse. But here I am on a deserted island trying to survive."

Instead of the truth setting them free, it raised more questions, creating distrust of each other. Their stories were unbelievable.

Though neither stomped away, the warm tropical air thickened with tension. The fact that not a single boat, plane or helicopter had been spotted during their entire time on the island, convinced JD they'd be stranded here for a very long time with no happy ending in sight.

Chapter Thirteen

Summer

Summer listened as JD shared his latest theory brought on by the lack of boat or plane sightings. When he added that he wasn't sure if they would ever leave the island, she broke down and cried.

"This shouldn't be happening. It wasn't part of my plan."

"Nor mine," he said, wrapping his arms around her.

His physical strength offered temporary comfort, but thinking of the future brought on uncontrollable feelings of anxiety. Being stranded on a deserted island only happens in movies and novels, not in real life.

An unexpected smile showed up on JD's face. "And I'm stuck on an island in the middle of nowhere, maybe forever, with Wonder Woman. Now that's a real man's fantasy."

She appreciated his effort to make light of the peril they faced. Still, staring out at the vast, never-ending body of water, she asked, "What's next? What do we do, JD?" Her words drifted out in quiet desperation.

"We have no choice but to proceed as if this is our home. If someone finds us, great. In the meantime, we survive. We have each other and we have him."

They looked down at Noodles' bright, shiny eyes. He was happy just to be with them, he didn't care if they were ever rescued. Oh, to be a dog. Having him took the edge off their frightful situation.

"I think we should explore the entire island. There could be more food or useful items here than we're aware of."

JD asked, "You didn't explore during those days before I arrived?"

"No. I had no reason to." She looked inland. "Besides, it's a jungle in there."

"Okay, then. Exploring the island is a great idea. But let's make a large SOS sign in the sand, in case someone sails or flies by. We'd hate to miss any rescue opportunities."

Summer and JD had a plan and a busy day ahead of them.

They followed the shoreline around the entire island. Summer wasn't up to any jungle exploration with bare feet and a nearly naked body. They'd save that for another day. Nothing they would call treasure had been found other than several weathered boards that had washed up on the south side of the island. The beginning of a shelter? Or firewood?

"You're limping. How come?" asked JD.

"Just a few blisters beginning to form. My feet are more familiar with water than sand. That last stretch felt like I was scraping my feet on rough sandpaper."

JD encouraged her to remain seated to give those sore spots time to toughen up before they became full-fledged blisters. "Hey, Ms. Biology Teaching Assistant. Any jungle plants around here that might have medicinal qualities?"

She perked up, suddenly in her comfort zone. "Yes, there are a few. We could make a painkilling tea and a healing poultice using banana shoots and leaves. Breadfruits are more for keeping people healthy than curing anything. If we stay healthy, we won't need cures."

He sat down, cross-legged, directly in front of her. "Tell me more."

She tried to, but speaking was difficult with his mouth over hers and his hands gently tickling her neck. Scientific knowledge about jungle plants was suddenly the furthest thing from her mind. She wanted this irresistible man.

Her protective fences fell, and her comfortable chrysalis dissolved. Yes. She'd risk a broken heart for JD. She'd risk everything for him. *Stop thinking. Just go with it.*

"I thought you were beautiful and sexy from the first time I saw you." He kissed her nose, her cheeks, her ears.

"You kept pushing me away."

"I regret that now. It wasn't just you. I've been pushing women away for several years. Thought they'd inhibit my career as a chef. Plus, I worked all the time. That's how I ended up here. My friends decided I needed a short vacation."

A far away look froze on his face. A look she'd never seen before, and that frightened her. She needed him in so many ways. What was he thinking? She waited.

When he returned from wherever his thoughts had taken him, he held her face in his hands and, gazing directly into her eyes, her soul, he swore he'd never push her away again.

"The truth is, I want to make love to you right here, right now, on the beach. But there is a greater truth. I have deep feelings for you. I love you, Summer." He watched attentively for her reaction.

Tears trickled down her cheeks as she threw her arms around his neck. He smiled, then eased her body down on the sand and hovered over her. He showered her with passionate kisses before rolling over and guiding her to the top position.

"We don't want your gorgeous derriere damaged by the sandpaper effect your sweet feet endured."

She giggled, but not for long.

His hands moved slowly down the length of her

back and then ventured lower. His gentle massage of her firm, rounded flesh sent currents of desire from her head down to her toes. She melted at his touch, and quivered when his tongue traced the softness of her lips. His kisses brought her body to an intense level of excitement. When he nudged her thighs apart, she gasped and arched into him. Their bodies swayed in exquisite harmony until the ultimate wave of passion swept over them.

Summer savored the feeling of satisfaction and love he'd given her. One of her unspoken fantasies had finally come true. She was the first to recover from the hypnotic effects of their lovemaking. She bolted straight up. "My Vacations Unlimited and your Fantasy Maker must have been in cahoots, don't you think?"

"Huh," he groaned, still working to regain his breath. " Has anyone ever told you that your epiphanies have unusual timing?"

"No. I don't think so."

"Well, just for the record, they do."

After laughing and hugging, they ate bananas and drank some water. Tomorrow was another day with plenty of work ahead of them.

JD

At daybreak, JD unwound himself from her sweet, lovely body, kissed her on the cheek, and whispered,

"I'm going for more water. When you're fully awake, could you weave another water container?"

"Yes, sir. I'm on it." Even with her eyes closed, she puckered her lips. He kissed them softly before she rolled on to her side and went back to sleep.

He told Noodles to stay with Summer, which he did. JD was impressed by how smart the dog was. "When I return, we're going fishing. Tonight we shall dine on something other than bananas."

Wearing only his shorts, he slung the old, beat-up backpack and the homemade water container over his shoulder and began jogging up the beach. Out of sight, he no longer needed to put on a happy face for Summer or Noodles. At times his smile was real, but only because the woman and the dog brought out the best in him.

Stranded on an island with next to nothing was upsetting, making him ill at ease. Even if Summer's campsite equipment still existed, a long-term stay would be difficult. Without it, survival was questionable. To say this situation was challenging for a career-minded, city slicker like JD was the understatement of the year. Far from his comfort zone and the amenities of modern society, he knew he must look as wild and scruffy as a caveman. A caveman without a cave.

"A cave. That's it! We need a cave." He shouted to the sky and immediately cut through the jungle heading toward the eastern side of the island. Maybe, just maybe, he'd find a suitable spot in the cliffs that was more substantial than anything they could build with palm fronds. The new project renewed his energy with hope. One cave, coming up.

Having climbed up and around the cliffs and traversed the island twice, he returned scratched, bruised, and exhausted. He saw the concern in Summer's eyes.

"What took you so long? We were worried sick." She threw her arms around him and the dog licked his leg. "You owe us an explanation," Summer said, pouting.

Prefaced with dramatic hesitation, he revealed, "I bought a house."

Her eyebrows shot up. "I see. And what did you pay for this house?"

"Nothing. It's a fixer-upper."

She punched him in the arm, laughing, and then showed him the containers she'd made. Taking his hand, she led him to the water and lifted the kelp net that held four flopping fish.

"Dinner!" They high-fived and kissed. Maybe being stranded wasn't so bad after all. There was something magical about appreciating four fish in a net. "You're becoming quite the island girl. I'd better build a fire so we can cook these guys, unless you'd rather see our new place first."

"I think eating some real food is a far better choice than walking to see an imaginary house."

"You think I'm joking?" He feigned shock and disbelief.

"You're not?"

He held out his hand hoping she'd take it. So proud of his discovery, he couldn't wait for her to see it. There was just enough daylight to get there and back. The fish would keep a little longer.

She frowned as they approached cannonball cliff. "We can't live on a cliff."

He smiled but kept silent. They pushed through some thick bushes to the farthest end of the rock formation. When he looked up, her eyes followed the trajectory of his glance. A delightful gasp escaped from her mouth at the sight of the cave. She scrambled up the gentle slope of the rock wall to get a better view.

"So, you like it?"

She nodded enthusiastically. "This will work. It's high enough to keep us dry during floods. And the rainy season could begin in about a week. But I like sleeping on the beach too."

"We'll do both. But we'd better get back and cook those fish. I'm starving."

The cooking fire's coals glowed in the dim light of dusk. Another busy day had come and gone. With full stomachs, all three were ready to settle in for the night. Noodles snuggled in between them, which was a first. And it was okay. JD rubbed the dog's ears and leaned over to give Summer a kiss.

"I'm glad you like the cave. We'll begin turning it into a comfortable shelter tomorrow."

"JD? We're still going to keep watching and hoping for a way home, right?"

"Yes, of course."

Chapter Fourteen

Summer

Summer used the small pot for gathering and carrying sand into the cave for the purpose of creating a sleeping area. Someday soon, she'd devise something more comfortable, but for now, the sand was softer than the cave's rock-hard surface and provided a touch of cushioning.

JD cleared out some of the bushes to make a neater, more accessible entrance while Noodles wandered around, sniffing the new location, and making it his own.

"Let's take a shortcut through the jungle and explore the area on the far side of the cliff on our way back to the beach," Summer suggested.

"Really? You're proposing an unnecessary walk through the jungle? In bare feet?"

"Yes. But I expect you to fight off all the dangerous creatures and falling objects."

She kept the mood light, not wanting to show JD how scared she was. Could they survive here? How would they cook after the lighter's fuel ran out? Or when the one and only knife became too dull to cut open a breadfruit or a fish? And, as much as she wished it were true, she knew humans could not live on love alone.

The walk back to the beach, though not a shortcut by any stretch of the imagination, proved to be interesting and fruitful. They found another rubber container from Summer's original campsite wedged between the low branches of a breadfruit tree. It contained one bottle of wine, a corkscrew, and several bottles of water.

They gathered bananas, their shoots, and their leaves for the purpose of experimenting with poultice making. Heading through a section of unfamiliar territory, the jungle became dense, and walking was a challenge. No more traveling three abreast. The dog and Summer followed JD as he led the way pushing vegetation to the side as best he could.

"Ow!" JD fell to the ground.

"What? What's the matter?" Summer asked, taking careful steps toward him.

"Stop right where you are or you'll trip and fall too."

Still, Summer inched closer and saw what had caused JD's pain—an old, half buried wooden chest.

They turned toward each other with wide-open eyes and dropped jaws. "Treasure?"

JD scraped away the dirt and sand and lifted it up. "Well, it doesn't weigh much, so it's not filled with gold doubloons." Gold would be of little value on the island anyway. They carried it back, vowing to pry it open later. Talking about what the chest might contain, provided a diversion, a little entertainment.

"From the looks of your toes and shin, I suggest we get to work making the poultice."

"Good idea, but where do start? We don't have a recipe."

"Spoken like a true chef. I'll experiment while you go soak your foot in some salt water."

Noodles ran ahead of JD and stood at the water's edge barking. His excitement was puzzling at first. And then, even Summer saw what had sparked the dog's interest and she joined them. The infamous crab-catching pot floated in with the tide, its lid still on tight. The dog kept barking even after they scooped up that pot. Odd. Perhaps an additional item was making its way to the shore.

Summer checked the kelp net while JD wrote the giant letters—H E L P—in the sand.

"We've got a fish in the net!"

"When everything is shipshape, I'll get a small cooking fire started. After we've had a fine meal, we'll check the coffer," JD said, winking and limping.

"The coffer?"

"Yes, wench. The coffer, the treasure chest. That's pirate talk, you know."

"I kind of figured that out, you old sea dog." Laughing, she turned toward Noodles. "No offense."

"Shiver me timbers!" JD continued.

She pretended to look annoyed. "Now I'm thinking mutiny."

Their bantering continued. "I don't think that's possible while marooned on dry land."

"When we first met, you were sophisticated to a fault. And now you're Captain Hook. Where'd that first guy go?"

"Not sure, but I'm hungry, mate. How about you?"

"Starving."

They split one fish three ways. The rest of the meal consisted of mashed banana and breadfruit cooked until it was crispy. The gray of dusk quickly turned to darkness. With only a faint glimmer of moonlight and the fading glow of the coals to light their way, they chose to end their workday. They'd save opening the chest for tomorrow. They drank the wine, perhaps their last taste of such a treat, before turning in.

Each with a hand on the bottle, they toasted. "To us."

Summer had more to add. "To our unique and creative talents. May they serve us well. Your turn."

"To survival."

Summer thought for a moment, then smiled. "To our love for each other."

"Yo, ho, ho!"

She shook her head. He was overdoing the pirate thing. "Cheers!"

Summer took the first sip and handed the bottle to JD. By the time the bottle was empty, clouds blocked the moon's light almost completely. Wrapped in each other's arms they shared gentle kisses and loving touches. Noodles, about three feet from their heads, lay curled up, in a rare deep sleep. They'd all survived another day.

"Mr. Middleton? Ms. Sinclair?"

Startled, they jerked to a sitting position blinded by the glare of a powerful light.

"Yes?" Summer was certain she was dreaming, but shielded her eyes from the intruding brightness anyway.

A large, uniformed man stood close by looking down at them. "Come with me, please."

JD stood quickly, took Summer's hand to help her up, but kept her safely behind him. Looking beyond the man, they saw some sort of watercraft at the shoreline, and the faint flickering of lights in the distance. "Who are you and where are you taking us?"

"I've come to take the two of you to that ship out there."

"Well, there's three of us." Noodles stepped hesitantly toward the stranger and took a sniff.

"My orders do not include the pick-up of a dog."

Summer could not hold back. "They do now. You'll carry three passengers to this ship you speak of or none at all." Silence hung heavy. Was she bluffing? Would she let their rescuer leave without them?

Even in the dim light, JD's skepticism radiated outward. "Before we go anywhere, I need to know whose orders you are following and why you arrived a week late." He stood firm waiting for an explanation.

"I don't make the arrangements. I've been told to tell you that the extra days were part of The Fantasy Maker's plan. The storm was not. We didn't learn of the unfortunate weather until yesterday. You will be compensated for any inconvenience the weather may have caused."

The uniformed man shined his light toward an orange pod-like vessel, its front end up on the sand, its rear end bobbing with the gentle surf. "Gather your personal belongings. We need to leave in five minutes." He returned to his craft.

JD pulled Summer close and held her tightly. "I suppose we should go, huh?"

"Yes, but not without Noodles."

"I agree. I'll carry him. He's all we need to take with us. We won't let him out of our sight, right?"

"Right. But don't you want the treasure chest?" Summer asked.

"Our rescue, our safety, and you is all the treasure I need."

Tears fell from Summer's eyes as they kissed for the last time on their island. They took one final look at what had been their home for two weeks. The place where they fell in love—against all odds.

"Come on, Noodles. We're going for a boat ride."

Chapter Fifteen

JD

After all three were settled in the pod—one of the lifeboats from the ship—Martin, their uniformed escort, answered a few of JD's questions. They learned that he had worked closely with The Fantasy Maker for several years, but he refused to reveal whether the Fantasy Maker was a person or a company. No name or gender was forthcoming. They were safe and heading home, but under a cloud of lingering mystery.

Motoring closer to the twinkling lights, they saw their ride home was a mid-size cruise ship. Neither had ever been on a cruise before, so while they were excited, they were also overwhelmed.

After transferring from the lifeboat to the ship, Martin led them to their stateroom. The stares from curious passengers sent chills up their spines. Perhaps, the unfamiliar air conditioning might have contributed to that feeling. Their tiny world had been hot and humid for the past two weeks.

Upon entering their temporary living quarters, Summer squealed with delight. "This is the most beautiful place I've ever seen." She opened the sliding glass door, breathed in the sea air and gazed out at the darkness.

"Mr. Middleton, here's my card. Call the number on it if you require anything, anything at all." This serious, uniformed man bent down and gave Noodles a pat on the head before he walked out the door.

They'd been assigned to one of the forward suites and given complimentary ID cards for charging anything they wanted while on board.

JD and the dog stood in the bedroom staring into the huge mirrored wall. "Hey, Summer. Come here for a minute."

She bounced in, all smiles and radiating with joy, until she saw their reflection. A scruffy, shaggy trio stared back at her. "That explains the strange looks we got." After a few seconds of pure shock, they hurried into the shower.

"Come on, Noodles. You too." The dog hesitated, then, after much coaxing, slowly entered the large shower, but sat in the far corner. "That's not going to do it, buddy." JD picked him up and held him close to the showerhead while Summer applied a small amount of shampoo.

Feeling clean for the first time in days, they covered up with the two plush bathrobes they found hanging outside the shower on the back of the bathroom door.

Summer dried and fluffed up Noodle's hair while JD opened the mini fridge to take a look. "Eureka! It's loaded. What can I get you, my dear?"

"Anything with carbonation." She chugged the soda down. "Ah, my energy is renewed."

"Yeah, I think Noodles' energy and needs are renewed too. Hmm."

As if on cue, an envelope slid under the door of the living area. Was it a general cruise itinerary or specific information for them? It was addressed to Mr. Middleton and Ms. Sinclair. JD opened it and they read the one-page note together. The first paragraph merely reminded them to use their ID cards for purchases and for reentry to the ship should they choose to go ashore.

The next paragraph contained vital and timely information. Martin had a special dog potty box built for Noodles, and it was located near the bottom of the ship, below deck one. A map was provided showing the inconspicuous, behind the scenes route they were asked to use.

The final line read, "Please check the bedroom closet before venturing from your suite." There was a handwritten P.S. at the bottom of the note. "The captain requires your presence on the Lido Deck as soon as your dog is comfortably settled back in your stateroom. Martin."

Summer hurried toward the closet. "Oh, my gosh! JD, we have clothes. Nice clothes. And luggage. Two bags with blue tags that have our names on them. I guess that means we get to keep the clothes." She twirled around with her arms outstretched.

JD stood in the doorway. "I love seeing you so happy."

"You're happy too, right?"

"Oh, yes, though none of this feels real yet. I keep hearing a voice in my head say, If it seems too good to be true, it probably is." He felt certain a negative side would make its appearance any time now.

Dressed in casual, stylish clothing, their first official dog walk was about to take place. They grabbed the map, which looked more like a complicated maze, and headed toward the "dog potty" area. They hoped Noodles would stay by their side and not choose to go exploring or for a swim. Due to the late hour and their back-alley route, it was unlikely they'd meet any other cruise guests.

Heading down the long hall, an unfamiliar voice called out. "Mr. Middleton, Mr. Middleton!" The young man ran toward them waving something red in his hand. "Sorry, I tried to catch you before you left your suite." The something red was an improvised collar and leash. He told them the costume designer for the ship's singers and dancers made it for the dog.

"Thank you. Thank you very much. Hey, you wouldn't happen to know where we are, would you?"

"Of course, sir. You're on deck eight."

JD laughed and winked at Summer. "No. Not on the ship. I mean where in the world are we?"

The friendly young man was the one laughing now. "We're in the Pacific Ocean. You've got ten more sea days with one quick stop in Hawaii before your cruise is over. Have a good walk, sir. Good night, ma'am."

Looking into each other's eyes, they exclaimed, "Hawaii!" They agreed that this cruise home was a wonderful way to be compensated for bad weather, but wondered if their trip planners were aware of the near death experiences that accompanied the bad weather.

After the long but successful dog walk, Noodles jumped on the bed, curled up, and fell asleep. JD and Summer walked out the door in search of the Lido Deck. Following the signs on the elevators and in the hallways, they arrived without any difficulty, but the beautifully lit outdoor area was empty. Not a person in sight. Had they arrived too late?

"Just like home, huh? Solitude, but on a cruise ship." He took her hand as they strolled to the railing at the far end of the deck. The stars twinkled and a gentle, cool breeze soothed their faces. His mouth met hers in a kiss that was an odd combination of passion and sadness. Would this be the end? Would they go their separate ways when the ship docked? He held her tightly and kept his melancholy thoughts to himself.

Suddenly, all the lights went out. Only starlight remained.

Summer snuggled closer. "Maybe we should go back to our room."

JD was not willing to surrender their loving embrace. "In a minute. Let's enjoy the darkness, the stillness."

In less than a minute, the stillness evaporated. Explosive, thundering booms and crashes took its place. The darkness disappeared as the sky above the ship suddenly lit up in a shower of multi-colored glitter. A spectacular light show continued as the romantic couple watched in awe.

Summer whispered, "Is it the 4th of July?"

"If it isn't, it should be." *Dear Fantasy Maker, whoever you are. Thank you.*

That night they rested well, and the next day they ate well, but stayed in their suite or on its veranda, exiting only to take Noodles for his walks. They weren't up to the constant hum of activity or socializing with strangers. More recovery time was needed.

They discussed their time on the island, the good, the bad, the confusing, and came to the conclusion that The Fantasy Maker set them up to be together as a couple, to need each other. He or she must have conducted a bit of research on each of them right down to their sizes and tastes in clothing. But why? Why do all that?

The days passed slower on the ship than they had on the island. It seemed they'd never reach Hawaii. Maybe if they'd participated in the shipboard activities the time would pass more quickly, but neither JD nor Summer was willing to leave Noodles alone.

They took advantage of room service, eating their meals in their suite or on the veranda. Together, they viewed movies on the big screen TV and soaked in their own whirlpool hot tub. They took the dog on long walks at least four times a day. Between walks, Noodles loved to sit outside and keep watch over the water. A clear, Plexiglas waist-high wall enclosed their private outdoor area, keeping him safe while he conducted his dog work with his eyes and nose.

They surprised themselves by preferring to remain on board during the hours the ship was docked in Hawaii. Soon JD would be home in Olympia and Summer in Sacramento. They'd return to their previous lives, jobs, hopes and dreams, not knowing what the future or fate might bring.

With dreamy, sad eyes Summer put her arms around JD's neck. "My love for you was not due to the desperation or fear I sometimes felt on the island. I'm sure of that now because I love you more today, right here on this safe and luxurious cruise ship."

"I feel the same way. I love you too." JD cleared his throat before continuing. "But we need time to get to know each other under ordinary circumstances. Our island experience was far from normal."

His comment brought tears to her eyes. He hadn't meant to make her sad. He wanted to do the right thing, the smart thing. Holding her close, the magic, the sparks that flew between them whenever their skin touched, canceled out all logical thought. And that frightened him.

His desires relished intimate contact with her beautiful, tanned skin. "You're so perfect for me," he whispered, guiding the silky shirt over her head and tossing it on the chair. She began to remove her slim-legged slacks, but he shook his head. He had other plans.

"Ms. Sinclair, relax. I'll take care of everything." He tickled her ear with his warm, tantalizing breath. JD's passion that had lain dormant within him for so long was set free. There would be no holding back. He gently removed her pants, enticing her with each touch. He scooped her up with his strong, muscular arms and laid her gently on the bed. He removed her sandals and kissed her toes, then ran his tongue around her ankles.

Her breath came in quick surrendering moans. "How can I relax when you are driving me crazy?"

He took a moment to look at her. Really look. Her natural beauty was obvious. He'd known that from day one. But it took two weeks on the island to understand the beauty in her heart and soul, and now he adored her. He took his time to explore, to arouse, to give her pleasure.

He held her face and kissed her as if his life depended on it. She met his passion with an urgency of her own. When he moved his hands over her body, caressing every inch of her like a sculptor shaping clay, she gave him a passion-infused kiss so intense it left him aching for all of her. Making love with Summer was like nothing he'd ever known or experienced. Though he was hot and aroused, it was so much more than that. The masculine heat and the fire traveled deep into his heart.

Summer

Summer awoke to dog breath in her face. Pleasantly exhausted by their intense love-making, they'd fallen asleep and neglected to take Noodles for his bedtime walk.

"JD. Wake up. Noodles needs to go out."

Looking at the clock by their bed, she saw it was 3:10 a.m. She tried a second time to wake her man, but with no success. Not wanting to clobber the guy of her dreams, she guided the dog to his side of the bed to see if a little dog kiss might do the trick. Yep. Worked like a charm.

"Hey, Noodles. Is it morning all ready?"

Summer translated the dog's wishes. "Not exactly, but we need to take him for a walk, now."

They dressed, then hurried to Noodles' special spot. Due to the early hour, they chose a completely different route on their trip back to the suite. No one else would be up and around this early, or this late, depending on one's sleeping habits. They took advantage of having the ship to themselves. They strolled, they wandered, enjoying the quiet.

They walked the length of each deck and estimated they'd traveled a mile, maybe more. Somewhere during their shipboard exploration, an unusual sign on one of the doors caught JD's attention.

"Summer, what do you make of this?"

They stopped and looked at the gold, engraved placard adorning the door. Rather than numbers like the ones on every other door on the ship, this one had words.

Summer touched them as she read, "Private Suite for TFM."

They stared into each other's questioning eyes, then looked back at the door.

JD spoke first. "Are you thinking what I'm thinking?"

"Maybe. But it could be The Fleet Manager's suite. Is there such a thing?"

"Or it could be Thomas Franklin Meriweather's suite or anyone having those initials."

"You made that name up, didn't you?"

JD nodded. All of their attempts to come up with sound ideas regarding the traveler in the private suite bordered on ridiculous.

"So, it must be . . ." JD paused, giving Summer time

to complete the statement with him. "The Fantasy Maker's private suite."

Slowly, they stepped away from the door, and then hurried down the hallway and back to their suite. Noodles loved the quick pace and trotted along happily.

Chapter Sixteen

JD

The chime for the ship's announcements rang loudly. Verbal instructions for leaving the ship followed. JD and Summer lingered lazily in bed knowing they'd not yet reached either of their destinations. When they heard, "All passengers must disembark in San Diego" they jumped up, threw some clothes on their bodies and the rest into their luggage.

They found two packets on the table in the living area with a note and a twenty-dollar bill on top.

Dear Mr. Middleton and Ms. Sinclair:

You're part of the blue group, the last group to leave the ship. Take these packets with you, but DO NOT OPEN them until you have completed the entire disembarkation process and you are on dry land. It was a pleasure knowing all three of you.

Martin

Was this standard procedure or more of The Fantasy Maker's games? They had mixed emotions when it came to this person, this entity that had arranged their island experience—an experience that included danger and deceit. They had fallen in love, but that could not have been part of The Fantasy Maker's original plan. No one could plan in advance for love. Sex, maybe, but not love.

Summer shook her head and looked into JD's eyes. "I hope these envelopes contain a rental car voucher. We have no wallets, no credit cards, no IDs, nothing but clothing, twenty dollars, and a dog."

"We can hope. I'm concerned that the budget for my fantasy might have exceeded its limit. But, Summer, you didn't apply for a fantasy. You applied for a job. When will you get paid?"

"I received an advance upon accepting the job, but the real money I'd needed to start up the savings account for my flower shop was to come after I'd completed my job successfully. That's where you come in. Maybe an evaluation form is in your packet, and once you fill it out giving my entertainment abilities an excellent score, I'll get that bonus."

They agreed that all of the events from beginning to

end were odd and unbelievable. Summer had never heard of The Fantasy Maker and JD was clueless about Vacations Unlimited. On one hand, they felt duped, scammed, taken. But on the other, they hadn't given any money to anyone.

"But we gave ourselves."

"You're right, Summer. We trusted total strangers with our lives; lives we nearly lost."

A ship announcement placed a temporary stop to their reasoning. "Blue group. Proceed to Level Three. Have your ship IDs in hand."

They gave all the other blue group passengers a head start hoping to avoid the commotion disembarking with a dog might cause.

After exiting the cruise terminal in San Diego, they spotted several benches facing the bay. JD purchased water for the dog and a couple of sodas from a nearby vender. Summer sat with Noodles, their bags, and the two sealed packets.

It was time. Time to open them. They prayed for some cash. Without it, they'd be stranded once again.

"Ladies first," he said, standing and then shifting his weight from one foot to another. His face withheld any hint of expression.

Summer unfastened the clasp and peeked in. "Looks like a letter and two envelopes." She read the short letter out loud.

· · ·

Dear Summer,

Thank you for completing your job requirements. Well done! We are terribly sorry about the storm. We did not intend to create an assignment so fraught with challenges. Even so, you far exceeded our expectations. However, you will not receive the bonus, but we hope you will find our substitutions satisfactory.

CEO of Vacations Unlimited

JD sat and placed his hand over hers. The joy faded from her face, leaving only a look of shock. Noodles licked her knee. "How could they do this to me?"

"I don't know, but you might as well open the two envelopes."

"You're right. How much worse could it get?"

Taking a deep breath, she looked into the thickest, heaviest of the two envelopes and then jumped up, screaming and dancing in a tiny circle. Noodles barked. Strangers widened their paths as they hurried by.

JD thought she'd been stung by a bee. "What? What?" He demanded to know.

"It's cash. Enough to get us home, I think." She sat back down and counted the money. One, two, three … forty-nine, fifty.

"So, you have fifty dollars cash?"

"Nope." She stalled, she teased. "Got fifty Benjamins."

Showing relief, she opened the second envelope. Its

contents produced a whole different demeanor that took her breath away. "There's another note."

"Come on. What does it say?"

"It says: Good luck with your new flower shop."

"That's it?"

"Not quite." She held up a check for $100,000.

They sat, mesmerized by the unbelievable amount of the check.

"Open your packet, JD."

"I think mine will contain something quite different. I wasn't working. I was given a free vacation. It's probably a bill." He maintained a stoic expression not wishing to appear foolish when the news wasn't good. At first glance, he saw a sheet of paper and two envelopes. That's what Summer had in her envelope too. Though he doubted he'd be jumping for joy. He read his note:

Dear JD,

Your fantasy is over. I hope you enjoyed it. You are now onto the next phase of your life. I wish you success. Will you find your happily ever after? That is out of my hands. It's up to you. I can't take credit for the dog. Perhaps he was a gift from a far more powerful benefactor than I.

The Fantasy Maker

. . .

They reflected silently on The Fantasy Maker's words until Summer blurted out, "Open your envelopes." He stared at them, but hadn't made a move. "JD? Are you all right?"

"Here," he said, handing the envelopes to her. "Take a look."

Without the slightest hesitation, she began the task. The thicker of the two contained cash. Five thousand dollars. Same as hers. Her jaw dropped when she peered at the contents of the final envelope. A short note was included. She handed the note to JD.

Puzzled, he read it out loud. The note contained one sentence: Be sure to invite me to the grand opening. *The grand opening of what?*

"I think this may shed light on that note." Gleefully, she handed him a check.

He stared numbly at the $200,000 check he held in his hand until his excitement broke free. "That moves up the opening of my small, gourmet restaurant by several years. This is a dream come true, almost unbelievable. Wait, maybe it's not believable because it's not real."

"Come on, JD. Let's believe it. We were chosen, we were lucky, and we fell in love. It doesn't get any better than that."

"Now that you've mentioned it, I think it does." JD's new expression had love written all over it.

"What do you mean?" Summer asked.

His eyes softened. "We have Noodles."

. . .

JD and Summer remained in San Diego to sort things out, deposit the checks into new bank accounts, and make plans for their future. San Diego was where The Fantasy Maker had chosen to drop them off. Perhaps this was where they belonged.

Grilled Wahoo With Taro And Papaya

Island Recipe by Chef, Paul Hodo

2 lbs. Wahoo fillets
Sea salt
Coconut milk and meat
Lemongrass
Banana leaves or kelp
8 oz. Taro root (small taro roots work best)
1 Papaya, skinned and seeded
1 Lime

Soak taro roots overnight in water.

Prepare the coals, taking them to a deep glow and white ash.

Submerge the fillets in a brine of sea salt and coconut milk for 30 minutes, then wrap in leaves along with the lemongrass.

Soak banana leaves in water for 30 minutes so they will be pliable enough to wrap the fish.

Lay out 2-3 layers of soaked leaves over the coals and when they begin to smoke place the wrapped fillets on the leaves.

Meanwhile, peel and slice taro root into ¼" discs and boil in salted water for about 20 minutes. When the slices are cooked through, but still firm, place them on the fish packets.

Papaya marinade: Grate or grind coconut meat, mix with lime juice.

Cut the papaya into cubes and marinate.

When the fish is white and flakes easily, remove from leaves, and serve with taro and papaya.

A Message from Paul

I created this recipe specifically to accompany Ms. Rohman's novel. I chose Wahoo (or Ono) because it is truly delicious and lends itself nicely to tropical preparation. If I were marooned on an island, I would still try to create a balanced and attractive plate.

All of the components are available at any good Asian market if not at your general grocery store. Feel free to modify this dish with a mango chutney or fruit salsa to complement the fish.

Should you be stranded on an island and happen to catch your own fish, a word of caution:

Ideally, the fish should be kept alive in the surf until the coals/grill are ready, then quickly filleted. Ono has a chance of carrying toxins, so care must be taken in cleaning. No eating the liver, the roe, or other inward parts. The fillets must be well washed.

Bon Appetite!

A Note from the Author

Summer's Island was the first book I wrote for the Fantasy Maker series though it has taken a few twists and turns and revisions since that first edition.

As a young child, I spent almost four weeks every summer on the east coast of Florida within walking distance of the beach. The character JD and I shared a similar experience where waves knocked us down repeatedly. I was fortunate to have my Uncle Bob there that day, and he rescued me. JD had to save himself, and that situation left him traumatized.

I recall walking on a beach in Mexico with my father many years later. Looking around, taking in the immediate environment, he'd said, "You know, I think if I were stranded here, I could survive. How about you?" A discussion of survival skills followed, and though I was in no mood for his topic, at the time, I never forgot that day. My dad lived to the ripe old age of 94 without needing to survive on a deserted island.

About a year after his passing, out of the blue, my mother said, "I should go on a cruise. That's what all the women do when their husbands pass." That was news to me. I'd never been on a cruise, but with my brother's help, we arranged such a vacation for mom. Since then, I've come to love the tranquility cruising on the ocean offers.

At the time, I had no idea these three events would one day resurface and spark my creativity. Thus, the birth of Summer's Island began to take shape. I hope you enjoyed reading this book. If you've read any of my other books, you know that I include a dog in every story. Finding a semi-logical way to add a dog to this book was a challenge. And then Noodles appeared.

May your adventures be memorable and safe.

Cricket

What's Next?

**More standalone stories in
The Fantasy Maker Series.**

AUTUMN'S GHOST

When Ranger learns of his odd inheritance, he enlists
Autumn's help to create the required haunted house.
October in New Hampshire is gorgeous, fun and games
for sure, but someone unsettles their lives at every turn.

Evil lurks.

Goodreads

BookBub

WINTER'S BLUSH

The Fantasy Maker strikes an agreement with Clay.
What's the catch? He must pretend to be someone he's
not. A quick read that includes mountain hiking, rescue
dogs, danger, and yes, some romance.

Thank You!

Thank you for reading *Summer's Island.*

Would you like to know when Cricket's next book is available? That's easy. Sign up for Cricket's (almost) monthly NEWSLETTER and you'll receive notifications of new books, giveaways, and other exclusive content. https://www.cricketrohman.org

If you enjoyed this story, please leave a REVIEW on Goodreads, Bookbub, or your favorite online retailer.Reviews are helpful to readers and appreciated by authors

About the Author

Cricket Rohman grew up in Estes Park, Colorado and spent her formative years among deer, coyotes, and fields of beautiful blue columbine. After retiring from a career in education, she became a full-time author writing contemporary fiction and western series and sagas about teachers, cowboys, dogs, lovers, and creative women inventing unique careers—just to mention a few.

**Cricket loves to hear from readers.
Connect with her via:**

Website https://www.cricketrohman.org

Facebook https://facebook.com/CricketRohmanAuthor

Twitter https://twitter.com/CricketRohman

Bookbub https://www.bookbub.com/authors/cricket-rohman

www.goodreads.com/author/show/112683.
Cricket_Rohman

Email cricketrohman@gmail.com

MORE BOOKS BY CRICKET ROHMAN

You will find the links and excerpts for all of Cricket Rohman's books
https://www.cricketrohman.org

The Fantasy Maker Series
Contemporary Adventures

SUMMER'S ISLAND
JD won a contest and ended up on a deserted island somewhere in Micronesia.
This is a wild beach adventure complete with danger, love, and a dog named Noodles.

AUTUMN'S GHOST
When Ranger learns of his odd inheritance, he enlists Autumn's help to create a haunted house. October in New Hampshire is gorgeous, fun and games for sure, but evil lurks.

WINTER'S BLUSH
The Fantasy Maker strikes an agreement with Clay. What's the catch? He must pretend to be someone he's not. A quick read that includes mountain hiking, rescue dogs, danger, and yes, some romance.

The McAllister Brothers Series
Romantic Western Adventures

COLORADO TAKEDOWN Book 1
This twisty cowboy adventure includes treachery
new love, family, courage, and amazing ranch animals.

MONTANA COUNTDOWN Book 2
A wealthy rancher's story-telling tendency entices two
eavesdroppers—a greedy criminal and a would-be
novelist—to venture to his Montana ranch to search for
his hidden treasure.

WYOMING SUNDOWN Book 3
Clint McAllister's challenge put his sons in grave
danger. Alice is furious about his foolish plan.
It was almost Christmas, a bad time for such nonsense.

WILD WEDDINGS Book 4
Family, fate, and formidable danger make loving and
laughing a challenge.
Trace and Troy love two city gals. Their love is strong
but their plan for new ranches and happy lives is
threatened at every turn. Who wishes them harm?

The Creative Hearts Sweet Romance Series
Creative Women Standalone Novellas

PHOEBE'S PHOTO FETISH

Phoebe Foxglove had three loves: Photography, Flowers, and Bobby.
Two out of the three served her well.

TINA'S TASTY TOURS
Tina has an impossible dream that comes with a substantial price tag. In the meantime, she works at the Punk Patio and a 1960s diner where she is required to look like Marilyn Monroe.

CAITLIN'S COW WASH
Caitlin feels trapped and out of place living in an old-fashion Leave It To Beaver household. Then, a perfect, win-win solution comes along—a cowboy named Cooper.

ANNA'S ANIMAL HOUSE
Desert gal ends up with a Pacific Northwest ranch where animals flock to her. She's a fish out of water but learns to cope, even thrive, in spite of an ongoing feud with the handsome veterinarian.

The Lindsey Lark Series
Fiction with Elements of Romance & Mystery

WANTED: AN HONEST MAN Book 1
Lindsey, a kinder teacher in survival mode after an unthinkable divorce, is brilliant in the classroom. Unfortunately, unwanted sinister challenges invade her

off-hours.

LETTERS, LOVERS, & LIES Book 2
Jake and Lindsey are in love, but so much stands in
their way.
Fortunately, they are smart, multi-talented, and they
love to laugh. Wendell, the 180-pound lovable mastiff, is
featured throughout this series.

HIT THE ROAD, JAKE! Book 3
Thrilling, romantic, and sprinkled with humor, this
novel reinvents the 'buddy movie' concept with the
written word... and a pretty woman. As Jake and
Lindsey travel from Tucson to Estes Park in their RV,
the dangers they face become deadly.

Saving Madeline
Standalone Contemporary Fiction
An entertaining story with humor, emotion,
and an unusual mother-daughter relationship.
Audiobook available too.

Christmas in the North Woods
A Children's Picture Book
Oliver Owl introduces the reader to his forest friends
who are busy rehearsing for the annual Christmas Song
Contest.
Audiobook available too.